The Best of Choeofpleirn Press

Winter 2024

Winners and Finalists for fiction, nonfiction, drama, poetry, and art published in our annual magazines in 2024

Choeofpleirn Press

THE BEST OF CHOEOFPLEIRN PRESS

Winter 2024
Fiction, Nonfiction, Drama, Poetry, and Art

Copyright 2024

Choeofpleirn Press Editors
James P. Cooper, Poetry & Art
Ruth J. Heflin, Fiction, Nonfiction, Drama, & Art

Choeofpleirn Press is a small, private press (501(c)3 nonprofit) publishing literary journals in northeastern Kansas at the foot of the Glacial Hills. Our goal has been to promote the best written and photographed creations we can in each magazine, which we have done over the last three years. We also publish select poetry chapbooks and books of nonfiction through our two book contests, the Jonathan Holden Poetry Chapbook Contest and the Kenneth Johnston Nonfiction Book Contest, held annually.

For the last three years, we have published four separate journals a year: *Coneflower Café* (Spring), *Glacial Hills Review* (Summer), *Rushing Thru the Dark* (Autumn), and the *Best of Choeofpleirn Press* (Winter). The Spring, Summer, and Autumn journals were each dedicated to one of three major genres of storytelling: short fiction, nonfiction, and drama. The top three winners of the five creative contests held by CP—the Derick Burleson Poetry Prize, the Ben Nyberg Short Fiction Award, the Phil Heldrich Nonfiction Award, the Susan Hansell Drama Prize, and the Mary Cassatt Art Award—are republished in the Winter magazine.

This issue of The Best of Choeofpleirn Press will be our last magazine publication for the foreseeable future because national granting institutions have long seen us as a small rural press not worthy of funding, so we are forced to reassess our financial strategies.

CP will continue to feature a poem-of-the-week on our website, www.choeofpleirnpress.com. And we will continue to host our poetry chapbook and nonfiction book contests. We are also experimenting with strictly online zines, such as our Harvest Harmonies contest this last October, wherein we selected poems matching the theme to create poetry-memes for sharing across the internet.

Readers can purchase individual digital issues of each magazine or book directly through our Bookstore. Digital individual issues of the magazines cost $6 each.

Readers who prefer print copies can purchase individual magazines from Amazon and other online bookstores (since *Rushing Thru the Dark*, Autumn 2023).

Writers can also purchase classified or photo ads to appear in specific books in an effort to promote their own works or websites. See our Promoting Writers webpage for details.

For permission to perform any of the plays in this magazine or for other question, contact Choeofpleirn Press through choeofpleirnpress@gmail.com.

Cover photo: James P. Cooper, "Glassy Hues of Sunset"

ISSN (Online) 2768-9999 (Print) 2768-7988
ISBN (print) 979-8-9911790-5-8 (digital) 979-8-9911790-6-5

EDITORS' NOTE

We have learned so much from our relatively short stint in publishing literary magazines, even though we walked into the project with a considerable amount of experience working with several different literary magazines over the years.

One of our major goals was to innovate literary magazines, especially the print ones. We knew online literary magazines existed, often called zines now, but we wanted to use the available technologies to make the print versions more beautiful and attractive to everyday readers, since the more a person reads, the better her/his/xis critical thinking abilities. And we knew Americans, especially, need a lot more positive exposure to "others" than most seem to be getting.

So we quickly changed from the smaller 6x9 size of magazine we published in 2021 to a full 8.5x11 magazine we published from 2022 to now. Since we wanted them to blaze with color both inside and out, we also kept adding on skills in order to achieve a great print magazine that will grace any office or waiting room in order to attract as many readers as possible.

We were happy to note that the magazines we sold through an arts center in Emporia, Kansas seems to have led to the *Flint Hills Review* adding more interior color photographs to their annual literary magazine.

As we learned to navigate the various online platforms that sell print-on-demand books, we learned how to use both Amazon KDP and IngramSpark to extend the reach of our works, which was necessary after we learned that small, local bookstores hate Amazon, so they refused to sell our magazines sold there. That lesson took an even deeper hold when we tried using Ingram alone, since Amazon pirates co-opted one of our magazines, selling it for $147 instead of its retail price, which meant we had to send "cease & desist" letters to the pirates and to Amazon in order to get Amazon to actually list the magazine at its retail price.

By utilizing online tools and programs, we also avoided the need to store large volumes of literary magazines to sell, since the online bookstores do all of that for us.

Ironically, while we developed techniques for minimizing the costs of producing literary magazines, including trimming publication time from sometimes years to less than a month, we never found any national grant giving institutions that took us seriously. Despite our growth in four years, we only received one tiny grant from the Kansas Arts Commission in 2024. Even then, the slowness of their payment disbursement meant we have not been able to use the funds we had planned on using to buy the advertising for which we had originally made the grant application.

When we realized that all our hard work was not being rewarded with sufficient funding, not through subscriptions, not through the contest fees we asked creators to pay, not through grant funding sources, not through donations, we made the hard decision to put our magazine publications, which are infinitely more time-consuming and money-consuming to produce than single books are, on hiatus for 2025.

Fingers crossed, we can win the lottery soon, so we can continue to publish these beautiful works of art and literature.

With Heavy Hearts,

Ruth J. Heflin & James P. Cooper, Editors

CONTENTS

The works in this magazine were all selected as winners and finalists by their fellow contributors. Herein are the best works we published this year, judged by their peers.

ALPHA CONTENTS
BY CONTRIBUTOR SURNAME

A ~~Poet~~ (Mom) Delivers Her Own Eulogy
1st Place in the Dercik Burleson Poetry Contest

Victoria James

I ask that you don't cry for me, don't drench your heart
with sorrow. If you could tap into my most sacred
memories, you would only smile.

Open up my mind to see Polaroids captured for safe keeping.
Find the joy there, see it filter life through my every vein.

I lived it and thank God I did.

I heard the warm soft "dada" every morning.
The flap of his little hand like bird wings, saying hello.
I watched dad light up anytime his son looked in his direction.

Aching knees bent low just to read a bedtime story —
interrupted by erupting "dada" and more bird wings.

Thump, thump, thump, thump
across the old hardwood floors of his sprinting crawls.

I witnessed dad hold an inconsolable baby
like it was his greatest treasure,
the world was pure in those moments.

I was part of creating core memories for my husband
and son — unforgettable joy we'd relive *(even in death)*.

Don't cry for me because how lucky *(God how lucky)*
was I to be given *any* time with my little family.

Let them come to you. Let them talk your ear off
about those memories. Listen to them choose you,
say your name. Let them wave at you like bird wings.

Because that's all I ever needed.

Goldfinch in the Pine

1st Place in the Mary Cassatt Poetry Contest

Jordyn-Elizabeth Pimental

Even the Geese Don't Fly in Perfect Vees Anymore
1st Place in the Ben Nyberg Fiction Contest

Patrick Manning

Early on Thanksgiving morning, Ed loaded his grandson Will into his Ford Ranger and drove south on route 219 toward the Allegheny National Forest.

Will twisted in his seat and watched the white smoke puff from the oil refinery. Even through the closed windows, he could smell the stink of oil. The day before, when Will's family had driven six hours from Philadelphia to Bradford, his father pointed out the welcome sign painted on the oil drums. Smirking, his father revised the message: "Cool town, warm hearts...but it still stinks like farts." Will's mother laughed but said, "Stop it," and his father turned to Will in the backseat and said, "Don't repeat that, Will!"

Now, alone in the car with his grandfather, Will heeded the advice.

Past the refinery, the expressway ended and gave way to a winding, two lane road. Will tried to count the trees that flitted past his window. The numbers quickly jumbled together, and Will squeezed his eyes shut against the growing tally marks in his mind. Ed mistook the boy's tightly drawn face for a smile. He felt proud of himself for taking Will out into the forest this morning. The idea had come to him standing at the kitchen sink, bracing himself for his daughter Joan and her husband Damien to arrive, half-listening to Belle, his wife, ramble off the list of dishes she would make for the holiday. He thought maybe he could show his city-raised grandson a bit about the natural world. About the order of things.

With conviction, he told Belle, "Tomorrow, I'm going to take Willy on a hike."

Belle patted him on the shoulder and smiled. "Willy would love that," she said, and she promised to keep everyone else busy with peeling potatoes. She had seemed proud of him, too.

Along the side of the road, Ed spotted a grove of black cherry trees. He slowed and pointed it out to the boy. Will opened his eyes again to look.

"We had a moth outbreak up here, and all those trees are going to need harvested." He lingered on the word *harvested*, and it filled the space between him and his grandson. Will turned the word over in his mind. He imagined rows of men in overalls marching out of the forest with wheelbarrows full of black cherries. A stream of deep red syrup followed them to the place where they flipped the wheelbarrows into a waiting truck. Will sniffed, convinced he could smell the sweet-sour of cherry pulp.

Ed said, "Same thing happened with the ash trees a few years ago. They came in and harvested just about all of them." Will tried to reconcile the ash tree harvest with the image of the cherry pickers. Now, the men in his imagination emerged from dusty clouds with wheelbarrows filled with ash, like coal miners marching out of their caves.

Will asked, "Do they burn all the trees?"

Ed turned the radio down to figure out what the boy was asking. Burn them? Had he heard right? He looked at Will, who sat looking out of the window with his hands white knuckling the shoulder strap of the seatbelt. He was a strange boy, Ed thought. Kind, considerate, but strange. They were calling it autism now, but Ed didn't believe it. The boy needed structure. Discipline. He needed someone to teach him how to be a man. The city was too claustrophobic, and the boy's father too indulgent. And Joan, it seemed, had abandoned her own upbringing and embraced Damien's urban extravagance. Once, when the boy was only two, Joan had taken him to the Philadelphia Museum of Art. Ed thought it was silly. *At that age*, he had said over the phone, *you can just take him to the grocery store. It'd be the same thing*. He laughed, and his daughter – suddenly – needed to finish the dishes and get off the phone.

Ed tried to imagine how Joan might answer Will now, wondering about burning all the trees. She usually mediated the conversations, like a translator fumbling between two languages that she barely knew.

Finally, Ed simply said, "No, they just cut them down. Harvesting trees just means you cut them down and turn them into lumber. To build with. Things like houses." Ed glanced at Will, then back to the road. Will looked satisfied with the explanation.

Although Ed was proud of himself for planning this outing, he also had to admit that he felt nervous to be alone with Will. The boy marched his two fingers like miniature legs along the base of the window and stared into the forest. Exhaling, Ed said, "You probably don't get to see trees like this in Philly."

Will offered a small shrug and looked down at the floor of the car. He was thinking of Fairmount Park and its dense forest that sprouted along the Schuylkill Expressway. He pictured himself in the tree house that cantilevered over the treetops, and he could smell the rot of autumn. From that tree house, the roar of the traffic hummed like a bird song. Will didn't know how to explain the smell and the sound to his grandfather, so he looked out the window and said, "My dad takes me to see trees sometimes."

Ed looked at Will when he spoke, but the boy's eyes were scanning the trees outside, like he was speaking to no one in particular. *For Christ's sake*, Ed thought, *Damien couldn't even teach his son to look a person in the eyes.*

He gripped the wheel and accelerated. His son-in-law Damien -- the stay-at-home dad, the med school drop-out, the social media guru, the man with painted fingernails and tattoos -- filled the road in front of him and took up all the oxygen in the truck. Ed cracked the window, and the breeze whistled in the cab. Against the chill, he gripped the steering wheel tighter and sped too fast through the intersection at Tack's Inn, the yellow blinking light only a suggestion. Ed had never felt comfortable around Damien, and the hike was as much about getting away from his son-in-law for a few hours as it was about being with Will. There wasn't one thing that had happened, no eruption of rage; just slowly, over the fifteen years Joan and Damien had been together, Ed's distaste for him grew and grew.

"When you say something, you got to look a man in the eyes, Willy." Ed scolded.

Will had heard this before—mostly from teachers. He tried to obey. He looked at his grandfather's eyes. They were staring straight ahead at the road and looked hard and veiny. "Sorry," he said instinctively. Will held his attention on his grandfather's eye and twisted his hands over each other again and again. He was not aware of his own rocking gently back and forth.

Finally, his grandfather looked over briefly to catch his gaze.

Is this what he wanted? Will stared at the top of his grandfather's nose just between the eyes like his therapist had taught him. Will told himself he needed a redo, so he shouted, "Sometimes I see trees with my dad."

Ed grimaced at the outburst. "Sit back, Willy," he said.

As the boy tried to settle into his seat, Ed swallowed his annoyance. Maybe this hadn't been such a good idea after all. There had always been a chasm between him and his grandson, matched only by the growing gulf between him and Joan. He wanted to blame Damien for it all. He had been a boyfriend they all thought Joan would grow out of; but there was the moving in together, the multiple relocations for med school and residencies, the wedding, then the baby. Damien had stuck around far past his welcome.

Ed realized, though, that it was too convenient to blame Damien for all of it. For starters, Ed hated long turnpike rides, nights spent under the glare of streetlights, and the loud neighbors at his daughter's South Philly home. Sometimes, too, he worried that his daughter had distanced herself because of his growing interest in politics. Joan was a pediatric cardiologist, and Ed felt that he had some share in her intellect and success. Because of this, he liked to pull her into political debates to prove his own intellectual acuity; she was kind and indulged him. He talked about the news of the day, but he could never quite articulate what all of it meant to him. It wasn't illegal immigration, or the liberal media, or vaccine mandates, or woke culture. Not really, anyway. But he could never quite put words to what he felt deep in his belly; it was always frustratingly just out of reach. And as he stumbled to explain himself, his daughter would grow angry or, worse, bored.

When she'd finally had enough, Joan would exhale and say, "Well, I better get dinner started."

Ed would say OK, and a few hours later send a text message of something off-topic, like a picture of the sunset, just to be sure Joan wasn't offended. She would always reply.

Ed accelerated a bit more. The speed calmed him.

"Grandpa Ed, it's kind of cold." Will hugged himself. Then, as an afterthought, he looked at his grandfather's eyes.

Ed rolled the window back up and slowed the truck. He said, "We're almost there, Willy."

Route 219 turned down a hill and, at the bottom, just before it crossed Elk Bear Run Creek, Ed turned off onto a small patch of gravel set back from the road. "I used to go hunting back in these woods," Ed sat for a moment and looked into the forest. "Long time ago it was an oil field, then the trees started coming back, and deer like young trees, so it was a good spot," he smiled, thinking back to when the forest was young. "Guess all the trees have grown up since then." He added, "Just like you," but Ed felt strange immediately after saying it; it was too cutesy, almost like it came from someone else.

Will didn't seem to notice. He unbuckled his seatbelt, pressed his nose against the window, and imagined the creatures lurking in the forest. He dispensed with the most likely candidates: deer, rabbits, maybe a bear. In the shadows lurked a centaur, the overlord of a world of elves. A dragon hid under the roots of the tree. The bare branches hid the fiery feathers of a phoenix as it surveyed its dominion. Will bounced in his seat; the boy's enthusiasm quieted Ed's doubts about the wisdom of this hike.

Ed got out of the truck and made his way around to open Will's door. "Need help down?" Ed asked.

Without answering, Will jumped to the ground and landed on all fours. Tiny pebbles stung his hands through his thin drugstore gloves, but he didn't say anything to his grandfather. Instead, he rocked from left to right and rubbed his palms on his pants. "I'm fine," he said and turned to the forest.

The trees were skeletons in the late November chill. Here and there an evergreen colored the forest with green, but mostly it was gray and jagged. The sky, though, was uncharacteristically clear and a brilliant blue. The morning light cast zig-zagged patterns across the truck. Will and Ed could see the trailhead, but it was marked with yellow hazard tape, tied around the trunks of trees, blocking the entrance. The tape looked stretched and weathered, but it hadn't yet been torn.

Ed reached down to help Will zip up his coat, but Will pulled back and bumped against the truck door. "I'm OK," he said. He pointed to the blocked off trailhead and asked, "Is it open?"

Ed shifted back on his heels and sauntered to the trailhead. There was a laminated sign nailed to the tree: **TRAIL CLOSED.** Over the summer, a strong storm had blown through, felling trees across the trail. Ed remembered the late-summer storm; there had been flooding in Bradford and reports of a tornado touchdown to the south. Traveling on the trail was unsafe, the sign said, on account of the trees, and some unstable ground along the ledge of a sheer cliff. But he didn't drive out here for nothing, Ed decided. And, besides, this was his old hunting area, a trail he had taken his own kids on for years, a place he knew well.

"Good thing for us," Ed said, trying to sound authoritative, "the forest doesn't close." He pulled up the caution tape and motioned for Will, who ducked under it and watched as his grandfather threaded his way through, careful to ensure his footing.

Ed breathed deep into his belly. The trail was narrow, but with the trees bare the path looked easy to navigate. He wondered why they had gone to the trouble of closing it at all; everything looked in good order to him. Ed zipped his heavy Carharrt jacket up to his chin. Though he seldom drove out this way, he felt a sense of control and calm in the forest. With intention, Ed reached out and pressed into the bark of a sugar maple tree. It had been almost a full year since Bradford Forest Company had laid him off. The company blamed it on the pandemic slump, but Ed knew it was a result of corporate reorganization after it was bought by a German firm. However, he had worked there for many years, so it was instinctive to imagine the tree as lumber. He looked up to the branches and read the ridges of the bark like Braille. *Not worth cutting it down*, he thought. *Couldn't get more than a few good planks out of it.* Will, a few yards ahead, had found a large stick and whacked it against the trunk of another sugar maple. Ed pushed himself off of the tree and followed his grandson.

Will darted along the trail and weaved a fantasy as dense as the forest. An Elvish spy had been sent by the commander of the Dwarf-Elf Alliance Army. *You need to get word to our troops in the west of the incoming attack from the Troll King.* Will leapt forward and whacked the tree once, twice, three times. The rhythm was predictable – a whack, a silent beat as the stick twirled above his head, then another whack as the stick landed against the tree. The vibration through his palm and up his arm was like a magic spell. The spy catapulted forward. In the tree limbs, however, a gryphon crouched with its wings tightly clasped. The elf saw it too late: he tried to cast a freeze spell, but the gryphon had taken off, made two circles in the air, and nose-dived toward the elf. Its talons sunk into the elf's shoulders and lifted him off the ground. *Where are you taking me!?* But the gryphon didn't reply. The elf unsheathed his sword and began to attack the gryphon in midair, landing blow after blow against the gryphon's leg.

"That's an oak." Ed called.

Will slowed his swings and reminded himself, *look at his eyes.* He found the spot where his grandfather's eyebrows met, but he could maintain his attention for only a moment. Then, Will darted forward again, in pursuit of some imaginary storyline.

The trail weaved through the trees and climbed steadily. Ed hadn't recalled such an incline, and he was breathless after the first half hour. A large rock jutted out from the forest floor, and Ed suggested Will play there for a couple minutes while he caught his breath. The boy leaped forward and swung his stick over his head. It landed with a loud crack against the rock and snapped in two. Will mumbled to himself the whole time. Ed could only make out the whispered refrain, "The sword of power is destroyed."

The boy stumbled backward as he played out the scene, but his foot caught a tree root and he fell. Ed moved toward the boy, but Will bolted up. His face was red with rage. "Why is this tree root here!" Will screamed. He attacked the root with his stick, and then turned his rage to the trunk of the nearest tree. It was no longer a game. "Stupid tree!" Will yelled, making animal sounds that echoed across the forest.

Ed watched the boy for a moment, confused about what to do and annoyed that this tantrum had disrupted the forest calm. Will was almost ten years old now; this behavior should've stopped years ago. "Willy!" Ed shouted. Will swirled and landed another angry blow. "Willy! Willy! Knock it off!" Ed had found his way to the boy and grabbed him by the shoulders. Will shrieked. His mouth agape, his teeth barred. Ed matched the boy's rage and screamed, "Stop it."

Silence erupted. The birds were hushed. The breeze halted. To escape the weight of his grandfather's touch, the boy plopped onto the ground. Will breathed through his mouth. "You're too big to act that way, Willy." Ed was angry, and he folded his arms and loomed above the boy.

Will studied the leaves on the ground. The veins were a secret map. He began piecing them together. He wanted to ask to go home. All the way home. Back to Philadelphia. To the forest along the highway. To the hum of his own street. But, his mother had told him to be good.

When he had whispered to her that he didn't want to go, she had said, "This means a lot to Grandpa Ed. Just give it a try. A new adventure. Who knows, maybe you'll even have fun."

He picked up two broad, brown leaves and held them together. A map! The elf had freed himself from the gryphon's claws, survived the fall from the sky, and now, there was a new map. A new path to warn the western troops.

When Will jumped up and lunged forward, Ed stood for a moment in the cold November air and shook his head. The boy acted like nothing had just happened. Not knowing what to say, he reverted to the common denominator. "I'm working up quite an appetite." It hadn't even been an hour yet, but he was thinking that maybe it was time to turn around. Ed *was* hungry, and he was thinking of the turkey and the pies. He thought of the sweet potatoes with marshmallows and the stuffing. He imagined his son-in-law kneading the butter and broth into the dried bread cubes and scooping it into the turkey. He could see Damien's hands–painted nails and wet with the work of cooking–and it turned his stomach. He closed his eyes for a second and breathed in the damp smell of the November woods, and thought of his wife, Belle, and his daughter, Joan. She was home, he thought. For the first time in years, Joan was home for Thanksgiving. And not only Joan, but his two other children and their families–all local to Bradford–would be coming over, and he could imagine the whole post-dinner scene. He would push himself back from the table, and he would update his children on his plans for fixing the roof on the garage. The house would grow colder as night fell, and Ed would show Will how to build a fire in the wood-burning stove. Will would marvel at the glowing coals and the magical warmth. Amidst the wreckage of dinner, the whole family would play Cinch, and his from-somewhere-else son-in-law would be confused by the rules and sit the game out. The grandchildren would get sleepy and doze off watching *The Grinch* in the living room, and Ed and his kids would drink homemade wine, and they would laugh big gut laughs about the one Thanksgiving when it snowed and snowed, and the oven broke halfway through cooking, and they had to pull the cover off the grill and try -- and fail -- to finish the turkey outside.

Ahead, the trail took a sharp turn, and Ed couldn't see much farther along it. Will had run ahead and was out of sight. "Willy!" He yelled. "Wait up, Willy!"

Will darted back into view. He said, "Just here, Grandpa Ed." He waved his arm forward. "It looks really different up here." He was off again, along the trail and out of view.

Ed tried to move quickly, but he could only get himself to half running. Every joint was a bit sore. Even pumping his arms felt like overdoing it. He wondered for a moment how he would ever be able to repair the roof on the garage. After the first snake curve of the trail, it climbed a bit more and then opened into a clearing. Ed saw Will standing on a downed log overlooking the open space. When he got closer, though, he saw that it wasn't just one downed log, but the entire field was a mess of fallen trees. The trail disappeared under the criss-cross of logs. Next to Will, Ed put his hand on the boy's shoulder and breathed. Will studied a large tree that had been pulled up by its roots; no longer hidden underneath the soil, it revealed a network of thick, knotty highways. The entire forest floor was nothing but trees. Why hadn't it been cleared yet? Ed couldn't help but quickly price the trees out for lumber. This could have made someone a fortune. He smiled and said, "How much do you think this is all worth?"

Will was so excited about the maze of logs ahead of him that he didn't even register his grandfather's question. With surprising confidence, the boy jumped from one log to the other. Ed called to him to be careful, to slow down, but Will wasn't listening; he was, by now, a few yards ahead of Ed. "Willy!" Ed yelled. The boy turned for a moment and smiled, then jumped to the next downed tree.

Without the trees overhead, the sun invaded the forest with an eerie brightness and spotlighted the latticework of wood on the ground. Will was back to mumbling to himself, jumping from log to log and hitting his stick against each of the downed trees with increasing force. Ed watched as the boy leaped to a new log, comfortable and confident in his footing. Will's comfort in the forest surprised Ed; he had to admit, a bit sheepishly, that this city kid knew his way around a forest after all. Still, though, he was lost in a daydream; almost ten years old and still lost in a fantasy world, muttering to himself about elves and witches as he bolted from log to log.

Ed waited for Will to turn back toward him. But the boy kept moving forward, further across the mess of timber. Will was already twenty yards away before Ed balanced on the first log at the edge of the path. "I'm coming," he called to Will. The wind was calm but cold, and the sun was bright, if out of place.

Will made it across the trees and stopped at the far edge to look around. "Where's the path?" he yelled back to his grandpa.

Ed planted his feet safely on two logs and tried to remember the curvature of the path. With the trees down, everything looked different, and he couldn't recall what came next. He was sure about a sheer cliff not too far off. And he recalled, maybe, a small clearing with an old oil derrick after that. But did the trail continue north from here, or veer farther east?

Ed looked over his shoulder for the trail marking. He pivoted at his hips, but the move left his feet unstable, and he lost his balance. His right foot slipped from the log and wedged underneath it. He fell backwards, his palms hitting unevenly -- his left on the ground, but his right caught the edge of a broken branch.

The base of his hand sliced open, and blood smeared over his palm. "Goddammit!" Ed shook his hand and tried to untangle himself from the logs. He inspected the cut. It hurt, but it wasn't too serious. He unzipped his coat, untucked his flannel shirt, and pressed his hand into the crumpled fabric. His head throbbed. He breathed deep. He leaned his neck back. It relieved the pressure. A little.

In the sky, Ed noticed a flock of geese. Recently, he had noticed that the flocks he had seen were misshapen. Instead of crisp vees against the blue sky, the flocks Ed had seen were sloppy. At best, they made haphazard U's. This flock was not only late in the season, but they flew in shambles. Shapeless. More a swarm than a flock. Ed squeezed his hand tighter. He wasn't sure if he was angry about the geese, or this failed hike, or his cut hand. He tried to gulp down the anger and turn his attention to the cut. He looked under the flannel and groaned.

Will heard the sound and glided over the logs to his grandfather. "Are you OK?" He asked. He put his hand on Ed's forearm. Ed glanced at the boy's gentle touch and snapped, "You need to stay with me!" Will shrunk back. "You got to learn to listen, Willy!"

Will sat on a log opposite his grandfather. Around him, the forest darkened. The trees sprang back up from the ground. Shadows grew. The space between him and his grandfather became overgrown with thorns and nettles. Will hugged himself. He thought of the word *harvested.*

"Stop that, Willy. Look at me when I'm talking to you." The boy was rocking back and forth now, holding opposite elbows in his hands. He looked everywhere but at Ed. Ed's anger wouldn't be swallowed, so he indulged it. It shocked the boy. Ed pointed skyward with his chin. "Look," he scowled, trying to get the boy back. "Look up Willy!" That got his attention. The boy looked up. "See that. Not even the geese fly in perfect vees anymore."

Will looked up at the geese. "Can we go back?" He felt guilty the moment he said it. Would Grandpa Ed tell his mom?

"Let's just sit a minute." Ed made himself a bit more comfortable on the log. Will watched the geese.

"It should be a perfect vee, to cut down on the wind." Ed tightened his grip on his cut hand and felt his pulse in his palm. He closed his eyes against the throbbing.

Will stood up, still staring at the geese. For a moment, he imagined they were rescuing the elf warrior, carrying him away from the western forces on their backs. The flock dispersed and dive bombed to confuse the gryphon, who was now on the scent of the elf. They were flying south, away from the western forces, in order to buy time. The gryphon tired easily. The geese, however, worked together to cut down on energy, taking turns carrying the elf, synchronizing flight patterns to reduce drag. Ed sucked his teeth and pressed harder on the flannel.

"Can I help?" Will asked, turning back to his grandfather.

"I just need a minute," Ed answered.

Will reached out and touched the flannel that stuck to Ed's palm. "If you want, I can take the pain away." Will pressed his palm firmly into his grandfather's hand. "You just need to push the pain out of your hand." Will looked into his grandfather's eyes. The pressure stung a bit.

"That's all right, Willy," his grandfather said, pulling back his hand and looking away, uncomfortable with the closeness. "That won't help right now."

Will blinked and withdrew his hand. He turned from Ed and looked up. With the trees downed, there was nothing between him and the sky. The geese still hovered above. If they were trying to write a letter, Will couldn't read it. He telescoped his hands and homed in on one of the geese at the head of the flock. He twisted his hands and zoomed in. The gray feathers sprouted like a forest—-an entire world soaring in the sky. Will scanned up the body and found the deep black of the eye.

Ed felt a ping of guilt over his outburst. He tried again. "Something must be wrong," he said. Maybe they lost the leader or something." He hoisted himself up and unwrapped his hand. The bleeding had mostly stopped now, but his palm was smeared in the deep red of a dried wound. "They are supposed to be in a V. Like this." He held his hands together.

Will turned to his grandfather and found the V shape through his telescoped hands. He panned up, pausing for a moment at his grandfather's eye: a brown marble hard as a bullet. Then, he scanned up and up into the sky. He found his goose still hovering. He zoomed in again. The black of the goose eye opened like a hole through the sky. It swallowed him whole—every bit. A bright blackness like closing your eyes in the sunlight.

The wind whipped past him. The rhythmic beats of the wings calmed his heartbeat. Will sunk his hands deep into the soft down of the goose's back, and the goose pushed up against his palms, welcoming the caress. The softness felt like relief.

Down below, Will could see his grandfather standing frozen with his hands in a peak. From way up here, the sunlight glistened off the flattened forest. It looked flat and glassy. Will stroked the slender neck of the goose and whispered, *it's not a lake down there. It's just a broken down forest*. The goose honked a *thank you* and twisted its neck to steer the flock away to a more plentiful landing spot. Will thought about staying. He imagined dipping his toes in the cerulean waters of the south and teaching the flock new letters, the whole alphabet, an entire story written in animal bodies in the sky. But he knew he had to stay.

Will fell back to earth, dropping his hands to his side and unclenching his fists, letting the few down feathers float to the ground. He watched as the geese scrawled new letters against the blue as the flock disappeared over the horizon, away from the flattened forest where he stood. He thought, *I hope they find some place soon*. Then, he noticed his own body, touched his belly, and felt a pit growing in his stomach.

"I'm hungry," he said out loud.

Finally, Ed smiled. "You and me both."

No. 492: A Flamingo's Tale
2nd Place in the Derick Burleson Poetry Contest

Brian C. Billings

Lavaca Bay. The gulls and I
have come to terms at last. Goodbye
to Sedgwick County Zoo. I guess I thought
I'd never leave, much less

for land so much like Zanzibar,
whose pools of blue-green algae are
still the waters that I sift in dreams.
The Bay has been my gift.

My place is not in hundreds here.
347, lost last year,
has come again in Carib form—a bird
who did not know the storm

that blew me south on unclipped wings
but comforts me when summer brings
a tempest, and my neck begins to shake.
My mate and I—twins

who did not share a bonding crèche
or capture or enclosure. Fresh
to pairing, faith in me defines his eyes;
their loyalty assigns

to me a deeper role than what
I had allowed—not loner but
commingler. Strain or skim or scoop,
I bend my beak to him.

Hide and Seek
2nd Place in the Mary Cassatt Art Contest

Karen Colstrom

Interior View
2nd Place in the Ben Nyberg Fiction Contest

Susan Harrison

The venetian blind that covered her sole window was askew. Amelia noticed it as soon as she entered her fourteenth floor Manhattan office. The cleaner must have been in a rush or was not concerned with perfection. But it bothered her, and she knew it would continue to annoy her until she fixed it. On most days, she kept the window covered. The view of the red brick wall of the apartment building on the opposite side of the street didn't tempt her. And even if she had overlooked Central Park, or a Noguchi sculpture, she rarely had the time to look up from her desk. Despite that, she did not lower the blind but raised it.

Across 56th Street, a window, its curtains drawn back, spilled light into the grey flannel air of a January morning and exposed the interior of a room, where a man lay in a semi-prone position in a railed hospital bed. The distance painted the stranger in broad strokes; a bald pate, eyes black smudges against parchment skin, a longish nose, a thin slice of mouth and a chin that disappeared into his neck. For a brief moment, her imagination, and it had to be that, summoned her father's face. Her dad had also lain in a hospital bed by a window, his view a cocktail napkin of St. Augustine grass and a magnolia tree. But today, he was nowhere on this earth. This month made it eleven years since he died in his home in Florida. Eleven years. It seemed impossible she had survived so long without him.

In all her forty-eight years, nobody had told her time dries your tears, but sorrow does not end. Mostly, her father came to her in the form of soothing stories of their shared experiences. But there were times, as in this moment, when his absence coursed through her with the sudden, sharp pain of a paper's edge slicing through skin. In an instant, she was back at his deathbed, the air redolent with disinfectant, her Dad's shallow breaths uneven and barely discernible, her throat dry from trying to voice the right words to pull him from unconsciousness long enough to utter one last expression of love. But God or nature granted them no reprieve and the warm hand she grasped turned cold and stiff.

Caught unprepared by this fragment of memory, Amelia felt a wellspring of sadness rise from deep within her. Even after she turned away from the window, it clung to her. But she had no time to indulge her emotions. Deadlines loomed on several projects, and soon the other attorneys and the persistent ringing of her phone would interrupt her. She shook off her unexpected wistfulness and attacked the tall stack of files and legal memoranda whose demands swept aside the specters of her father and the man in the window.

At 6:30 p.m., she closed her book of Securities and Exchange regulations, placed copies of completed legal memoranda in folders and filed them, put a list of unresolved client questions on the upper right corner of her desk, and closed out her computer. As she sat there, unshielded by her work, the face of the man in the apartment, or was it her father's face, appeared on the window glass next to her reflection. With lifelike stubbornness, this vision refused to leave. It made her dizzy, not physically but mentally. For a while, place and hour were forgotten and her whirling head kept her seated at her desk. Then some internal alarm made her recall her dinner date with her best friend, Heather. Thank God. Her friend would be the perfect antidote to the strange vertigo that had unbalanced her.

Walking into *Oscar's*, Amelia spotted Heather at a booth near the back, a bright parrot among the drab pigeons and sparrows from midtown professional offices. As Heather stood to greet her, Amelia took in her outfit: a lime green floral-print tunic pulled close to her waist by a wide leather belt, baggy navy pants, a large-linked gold chain at her neck, big gold hoops in her ears and chunky, black patent leather boots. She had colored the premature white streak in her brown hair blue, an improvement on the purple shade she'd sported the last time Amelia had seen her. Heather's eyes traveled over Amelia's body as she plopped herself into the seat opposite her.

"Whenever I look at you, I feel like such a failure," Heather said. A frown marred her smooth forehead. "We've known each other, what, almost thirty years, and despite all my efforts, you still dress as if you've arrived to draft my last will and testament."

"That's rather harsh, don't you think? I'm an attorney for a financial services company, while you're a buyer for a chain of chic women's wear boutiques."

"Start a revolution. Explain to those in power a little color and style doesn't affect how your brain functions."

It was an unresolved debate they'd had many times. Amelia had never been able to dissect the thought process of men of a certain age. Years ago, top executives, all male, drafted and distributed a detailed written directive that banned female attire they judged too attention- grabbing for the office. No matter how often HR suggested they amend that part of the job manual to give women more choices, not one letter of it changed. Amelia had been furious at their paternalistic attitude. The executives' fake concern, evidenced by the dress code, was laughable since management looked the other way when a man subjected a woman to a "friendly" hand that slid from shoulder to buttocks of her properly suited and buttoned-up torso.

Until recently, if a woman complained about a man's conduct, he was only given a warning and required to attend sexual harassment training. What a joke!

It was difficult to explain her reality to Heather. Most of the people in her company, including senior management, were women, and so Heather expected the continued advancement of women's equal participation in the workplace, while Amelia was still able to cite examples of subjugation.

"Honestly, Heather, it makes no sense for me to spend energy on a non-starter."

"Okay, you win. I'm too parched to continue this discussion. How about a drink before we order? As I recall, it's the one thing we always agree on."

"Very funny." Amelia smiled at the memory of their early disputes. If Heather hadn't lied on her dormitory questionnaire, they never would have become friends. Because they both asked for a girl who was neat, and an early riser, the college matched them up. It took Amelia less than a week to figure out her new roommate had neither of these traits.

When questioned about the disparity between her housing form and her obvious habits, Heather had been unashamed. "Just because I'm not tidy doesn't mean I don't appreciate a tidy room, and I needed someone who'd wake me up if I slept through my alarm."

They survived their first semester in close quarters because of Heather's unwavering belief they'd be best friends. By then, Amelia had discovered Heather's irresistible sense of fun, generosity, and kindness more than compensated for the attributes that irritated her. They remained roommates throughout college, rented an apartment together in New York City when they started work, and served as each other's maid of honor at their weddings. Years of shared dinners, family trips and incalculable hours on the telephone had created their symbiotic relationship. Amelia told Heather almost everything. Yet, now, she wasn't sure she could disclose her preoccupation with the man she'd observed through her window. It would sound bizarre, and she was afraid Heather would be dismissive. She tried to put him out of her mind and concentrate on what Heather was saying. But the unaccountably familiar man stole her attention and wouldn't be pushed aside. Unrehearsed words tumbled out of Amelia's mouth.

"My father has been on my mind all day."

"Your father was a great guy. He was one of the rare parental types who really got me, you know?"

Amelia laughed. "He always appreciated you. I guess you appealed to his sense of humor."

"It's possible. I'm sure it pleased your father that he's been on your mind."

Amelia tried to keep her expression neutral and resist the impulse to make a pointed comment. Heather not only accepted the existence of heaven and hell but was convinced the departed watched over the living. After death they transformed into personal angels with the ability to read minds and communicate through signs if you were astute enough to interpret them.

Amelia wished she shared her friend's beliefs. It would restore her spirits if she accepted that her father, in whatever form, could read her thoughts and divine the sentiments she'd struggled but failed to voice when he was alive. But this scenario was someone else's fantasy.

"I saw a man today who looked a lot like him. Well, maybe not. It was from a distance, so I might have been mistaken. But I can't seem to get him out of my mind."

Heather's eyebrows went up and her eyes focused on Amelia. There was no laughter or teasing in her voice when she said, "Perhaps your father is trying to send you a message. Have you needed comforting lately?"

"I don't believe in messages from the dead and I've been doing just fine, thank you."

"I know you accept the existence of God which depends solely on faith. Is it such a leap to maintain the souls of the departed can connect with us?"

"It's not the same thing."

"Why, because it was never part of what your parents or your church taught you?"

"There's a limit to what I'll accept without scientific evidence."

"So, you hold that science can solve all the mysteries of the universe?"

"No, I don't think the ability of the human brain stretches that far."

Heather smiled. "That's a big concession for you."

"It's the two glasses of wine talking," she said and then changed the subject. It wasn't until they were pulling on their coats to leave that Heather circled back to Amelia's confession.

"You know, your interest in the man you saw doesn't mean you qualify for a psych exam. I understand I'm not your yardstick for measuring rationality, but to me, your reaction is reasonable."

Amelia thanked Heather with a quick hug. Later, she wondered if Heather's words had given her permission to act uncharacteristically.

In the following days, it became a morning ritual for Amelia to look at the apartment across the way to check on the man in the bed. She would turn off the overhead light and stand so close to the window she could feel the cold radiating off the glass, all to get the best possible view. Amelia made a rule that she would confine her spying to the brief period at the beginning of the day when the office was empty of activity. In this way, she could hold on to the illusion that she was not crazy, merely curious. Then late one afternoon, when the reflection of the sun's rays no longer obscured the interior of the stranger's apartment, she interrupted her work just to stare at him. She strained to see if a visitor had pulled up a chair next to his bed, or if he held a phone up to his ear or worked on a laptop. Any of those activities would have dispelled the concern she felt for him. But he always appeared to be alone, and every day the position of his body changed very little.

Amelia wondered what he contemplated during such enforced inactivity. Was he sick with a survivable disease, or was he dealing with a terminal condition? And if death is your intimate companion, what does your mind latch onto—images of the past, the present moment, or queries about the unknowable future? With her eyes fixed on this stranger, she began to suffer from double vision as her father's face overlapped his, and the present merged with the past.

Twenty-two days before her father died, she had spent a week with him. It was heavy coat and gloves weather in Connecticut, but warm in Naples, Florida, where her parents lived. They had moved after she finished college and left home. Even though she'd visited them many times over the years, she wasn't comfortable in their current place. She forgot where to find tableware or pantry items in the kitchen, and the sofa, chairs and mattress no longer fit the contours of her body. The furnishings of her childhood had been replaced with matching contemporary pieces that always reminded her of a magazine spread or a store display; the wood, glass and fabric surfaces devoid of the scratches, worn spots and stains that once illustrated their family history.

Amelia might have enjoyed the warm weather, but she only went outside once; a trip to the grocery store with her mother. Inside the house, vents spewed conditioned air chilly enough to require a sweater. Beside her parents, the only person she saw was the home health care nurse who came in to help bathe her father and administer medication. Amelia slept in the guest room with her mother who snored loudly from a twin bed a foot away from her own. Late at night, unable to sleep, she went into her parents' bedroom just as she had as a child when she was shaken awake by a bad dream. As soon as the door swung open her Dad's eyes found her.

"I'm sorry did I wake you?"

"No, I was just lying here thinking."

She hoisted herself up onto the hospital bed, eased her weight down on the mattress, and stretched out next to him. His body emanated a cloying floral scent, his breath was fetid and the linens smelled of bleach. Once, her Dad had given off the scent of Old Spice aftershave and peppermint Lifesavers. She closed her eyes and tried to imagine they were back in a time before his illness. But the surrounding darkness worked its way inside her, and she couldn't retrieve that sheltered child. Lying next to him no longer dispelled her fears, as it had so many years ago, it only heightened them. Maybe it was her turn to provide strength and solace.

"A penny for your thoughts" Amelia said, an expression her father always used when he caught her staring into space.

He expelled a breathy chuckle she heard only because she was so close to him.

"Your mother's going to need you when I'm gone."

The response closed Amelia's throat, and she had to force out a reassurance. "You don't have to worry; I'll look after her."

Amelia held her breath and waited for him to pursue the subject further, but he was silent. There was still so much to talk about, the provisions of his will, his trepidations and regrets, their shared memories, what his life had meant to him, to her. Amelia's yearning to hear what her father had to say and to respond battled with her disquiet over dealing with such a discussion. She considered picking up the thread of his statement and continuing on, but she held back because he had always been the teacher and she the student, he the leader and she the follower. It was impossible for her to imagine usurping his role, and it seemed particularly cruel to do it now.

The quiet in the room became burdensome. She realized if they were to have this conversation, she would have to initiate it. Unfortunately, she was handicapped by her fear of breaking down and the very traits her father had passed on to her.

Her Dad was not a talker. He had always communicated tenderness or concern by the expression on his face, a hug, driving forty-five minutes to bring her a can of gas when she was stuck on a country road, displaying her report card on the refrigerator, and slipping extra cash in her pocket as she left after a visit. During those nights together, it was her fault they had talked at length about nothing – the weather outside, had she been to the pool, her son's basketball game, the book she was reading, the flowers in her parents' garden, going on and on about unimportant matters. And during those dark hours, what she wanted to say played in a mental loop, background noise to the mundane; "I'm not ready for you to go, You've been the best father in the world, I still need you, I can't manage without you, I love you," but the words remained stored in her head.

The doctors said nobody could predict how many months he had left, and she convinced herself there would be other opportunities to reveal her feelings. If she had known it was the last time they would talk, she might have found a way to express herself. Now, she felt she'd cheated both of them. If she had shared one meaningful thought or emotion, perhaps she would not be left with the loose ends of regret.

January was almost gone. At lunchtime, Amelia left her container of vanilla yogurt and an apple in the break-room refrigerator, walked to *More Than Sandwiches* on 6th Avenue, and picked up a salad. The restaurant wasn't a place she frequented, but to get there she had to walk down 56th Street. On the way back to her office, she halted at the entrance to the old man's apartment building. Movers were carrying in furniture. They had propped both the exterior and interior doors open, and with no hesitation she walked in behind them. One of the workmen held the elevator for her. She accepted the invitation, squeezed in between the wall and a teak buffet, and pushed the button for the fourteenth floor.

There was nothing unique about the empty, beige-carpeted hallway with identical numbered entries on her left and right. The only sign of occupancy was the smell of onion and garlic from somcone's cooking. Starting at the hall's near corner, she counted the doors facing 56th Street and tried to figure out which one opened into the room she had viewed from her office. Like the peal of a bell, the phrase "what am I doing here" repeated in her head. Had she developed an unhealthy obsession? The notion made a chill run through her. With quick steps, she rushed to the elevator. As she passed through the lobby, she noticed a bulletin board covered with advertisements and tenant posts. One sheet of paper stood out. Written in elegant long hand, it stated, "Wanted: a bibliophile to read to an older gentleman for forty-five minutes, four days a week." Underneath the job description was the apartment number, 1410, and a request to respond to Arthur Stevenson with his email address.

Amelia was almost positive 1410 was the residence that offered her a view of the man in the hospital bed. She reread the notice, impressed by the fine script and how he had narrowed the field of respondents by using the term bibliophile. Her father had been a voracious reader of novels, biographies, and books on business practices, and they had always traded and discussed books when she visited him. She strained to remember if he read or was read to in his last days. At that moment, her father's end-of-life practices gained exaggerated importance, but her memory failed her. It might be why the simple desire of this Arthur person called out to her. She removed her phone from her purse and snapped a picture of the advertisement.

On the way home on the train, Amelia opened her iPad and struggled to draft a response to Mr. Stevenson's flier. And as she wrote and deleted and rewrote, she found no valid reason to want to read to a stranger, even if he was the man in the window. She wasn't a person who volunteered for organizations that helped others, or someone who had free hours to fill, yet... .

After several attempts she came up with wording stripped down to its essence. "I am a bookworm with good verbal skills and would be available to read Monday through Friday around midday at a mutually agreeable hour." She reviewed her response a few times. She wondered if it would be enough to get her an interview. It was all she wanted, just to meet him. Once she told him her availability would always be subject to unexpected work demands, she was sure he would reject her, and save her from whatever strange impulse had infected her. Yet if that was how she felt, why do it at all? Moments ago, a decision had comforted her, but now her confidence turned to uncertainty. She pulled back the finger poised to hit send and left her reply in her draft file.

When she stepped off the train, the platform was covered with a thin, slick layer of snow and flurries thickened into a fine net curtain. She and her father had loved to walk in the snow the minute a storm ended, particularly if it was early evening when everyone else would be snug inside their houses. Before they ventured outside, they would layer on long underwear, flannel shirts, sweaters, jeans, down jackets, wool knit caps, gloves, scarf, and fleece lined boots. One step beyond the doorway, the cold air slapped them in the face and turned their exhalations into smoke signals. She had loved the contrast between the warmth of her body and her cold cheeks. She and her Dad always held hands; insurance against frostbitten fingers her father would say when she was at an in-between age, and he sensed her hesitation. Before they took their first steps, they looked out over a neighborhood cleansed and softened by the storm. The uneven ground before them was hidden by an unmarked surface of stacked crystals, glittering in the circles of light cast by the streetlamps. Icy air worked its way into any gaps in sleeve cuffs and jacket collars, awakening them from their reverie.

"Let's get moving," her father would say. Tramping into the powder, she and her Dad pretended they were explorers journeying through virgin territory, the dark hollows of their footprints acting as blazes to mark their trail home. Amelia shook her head. Now what had made her remember that? As the snowflakes hit the warm skin of her face, she felt them turn into teardrops.

The next morning, an hour before her alarm was due to buzz, she dreamt she was at the airport about to depart on a flight for a visit with her father. She walked up to the gate for her flight and discovered they'd changed it. She arrived at the new gate and found another gate number posted, and at the next gate the sign board listed a different gate. As her flight's departure time got closer and closer, she became frantic. She continued to run to each location until she woke up in a panic. In the second before she was fully conscious, her belief she'd missed her plane and her chance to be with her Dad made her forlorn. She glanced over at her husband's sleeping form and eased out of bed. Tiptoeing into the next room, she picked up her iPad. With no internal debate over whether her decision was normal or abnormal, she opened her draft email and hit send.

Two days later, Amelia heard from Arthur Stevenson. He asked her to come for an interview the following day at 12:30 p.m. It surprised her because she'd already convinced herself he had rejected her application. The morning of her appointment she found it impossible to focus on anything for more than a few minutes. And when the time came for her interview, she felt as if she had teleported to Mr. Stevenson's doorstep, for she had no memory of the walk from her office to his building.

Now, buzzed in, she hesitated in front of the elevator and gnawed on a fingernail until the coppery taste of blood filled her mouth. An argument in her head grew heated—proceed, don't proceed; sane, insane. She took a deep breath, rode up to the fourteenth floor and knocked on the door to 1410. A male nurse in green scrubs answered the door and escorted her into the living room, which had cream-colored linen wallpaper and a tasteful mix of English and French antiques. An oversized oriental rug in maroon, cream and black almost covered the wood floor. Against the far wall was an enormous mahogany cabinet with beveled glass doors. Behind the panes she saw shelves crowded with books, their multi-colored spines resembling a pop art painting. A man sat in a brown leather, tufted wing-back chair with his legs stretched across a matching ottoman, tasseled loafers on his feet. He wore grey slacks and a glen plaid long-sleeved shirt topped with a charcoal wool vest. A fringe of silvery white hair encircled his bald head.

"You must be Amelia. Thank you for coming. Please make yourself comfortable." He gestured to the chair next to him.

"It's nice to meet you, Mr. Stevenson."

"Please, it's Arthur."

As she settled herself, she glanced at the shadow box end table between them. Bookmarks, expensive by the looks of them, lay on royal blue velvet lining the bottom of the case.

"I see you've noticed my collection of antique silver bookmarks. The oldest is English from the 1860s."

"They're beautiful. Do you ever use them?"

"I used my first acquisition for a while, but once I began a serious collection, I've kept them all under glass and switched to cloth or paper place holders for daily use."

"If you don't mind my asking, which one was your first purchase?"

"The saber in the center. As a child, I loved stories of knights and sword play. My favorite books were *Ivanhoe,* and *King Arthur and His Knights of the Round Table.* I even took up fencing when I was in college, and during my working years I belonged to the New York Fencers Club. I found it helped me in my job as an architect."

"How so?"

"Fencing is often referred to as physical chess for an excellent reason. There is logic and strategic tactics behind each of your moves, and you have to make instantaneous observations of your opponent's physical skills and the psychology of his fencing personality. In a sense, it's not so different from dealing with clients, contractors, and planning commissions."

"That's fascinating. Would I be familiar with any of the buildings you designed?"

"Wait a minute, who's interviewing whom here!" Arthur smiled. "Why don't you tell me a little about yourself?"

When Amelia told Arthur she was an attorney, he nodded.

"Ah, that explains the cross-examination." His dark brown eyes studied her for a moment and then he continued with his questions. Where was she from, was she married, any children, her favorite books, and had she ever read to anyone other than her boys? Then, he had her read a page from a biography, *The Years of Lyndon Johnson*. At home the previous night, she had spent an hour reading aloud for such an eventuality, yet she heard a slight quaver for the first sentence or two before her voice smoothed out. Her desire to be not only passable, but applause-worthy, puzzled Amelia. All Arthur probably wanted was someone with a reasonably clear, pleasant voice that didn't grate on his nerves.

"Very nice. Your verbal skills are as advertised."

Afterward, he proposed a schedule that was good for her with flexibility about arrival times as long as she came earlier than two o'clock. Their conversation had dispelled Amelia's unease, and she found herself drawn to him.

On her second visit to the apartment, Arthur asked her to look through his books and pick out something she'd enjoy. It was a simple task, but it made her tense. For some reason, when in his presence Amelia had a childish urge to please. Would Arthur see her in a particular light based on her choice? This idea of being judged unsettled her.

"I can only guess at what you might be in the mood for or have read in the last year or so. Wouldn't you prefer to choose?"

"Don't worry, I'll tell you if I'm not satisfied with your selection. These days, it's difficult for me to make quick decisions."

His books were familiar to her. Many had had a place on shelves and tables in various rooms of her parents' home. Arrayed in front of her were the works of old companions: Gore Vidal, E.L. Doctorow, John LeCarre, Mary McCarthy, Philip Roth, James Baldwin, John Irving, and Daphne DuMaurier among others. There were also current gems, and a novel she had purchased and loved caught her eye, *A Gentleman in Moscow*. She pulled it out and held it up.

"Have you read this one?"

"I haven't gotten to it yet. It was a gift from my son last Christmas. What's it about?"

"It's set in Russia and begins in 1922, when a Bolshevik tribunal sentences Count Rostov to house arrest for life in Moscow's Metropol Hotel."

The description elicited a laugh from Arthur. It wasn't a feeble laugh, rather the kind that rises above the noise of a crowded room and makes heads turn. And it made Amelia want to join in.

"Well, I suppose I can relate to a person who is unwillingly confined. I'm curious about how someone, even a fictional character, handles such a situation. Your selection is approved. Shall we begin?"

Amelia hadn't read aloud since her two sons were six or seven. She had forgotten how different it was from reading to yourself. She'd never been able to act out the stories the way her father had. She remembered his use of sound effects to imitate a train's whistle, a barking dog or the whooshing of the wind, and how he gave each character a unique voice. Reading to an adult is not the same. Her task was to mind the punctuation in order to maintain the meaning and rhythm the author had established. Sometimes when she glanced up, it surprised her to see Arthur instead of her Dad. Now, his eyelids were closed, and a slight smile pulled up the corners of his mouth. She wondered if the sound of her voice had put him to sleep, but when she paused, Arthur's eyes opened wide.

"Being read to brings me back to my childhood. It's a forgotten pleasure, in the same category as the anticipatory static of a needle on a record before the music begins, or the sensation I get when the nib of a fountain pen forms letters on paper. You know, I really miss the hand-written personal messages I used to receive. These days when you open your mail, there is nothing to look forward to but bills and junk."

"I understand just what you mean, a note or letter was always a wonderful surprise, and it turned an ordinary day into something special. Our mail always came in the afternoon, but I would prolong my anticipation by waiting until after dinner to tear open the envelope."

On the train home, going through her email, she recalled her conversation with Arthur about letters. It reminded her of the last letter she wrote to her father. She and her husband had been about to leave on a trip to Japan and five days prior to their departure date, a Boeing 737 crashed, killing all the passengers. They were scheduled to travel on the same model Boeing. Flying under any circumstances made her anxious, and that evening a nightmare haunted her. In her dream she was on board the plane, her upper body bent over her knees in the brace position, counting the seconds until impact as the aircraft nose-dived toward the Pacific Ocean. Once awake, she was consumed by an urge to update their wills and send a long overdue letter to her Dad.

Amelia's two-page letter included a response to something her father said to her a few months before. She'd been talking about how terrific a friend's husband was with their new baby. He said he was sorry he hadn't been a "liberated" man. It was not something Amelia had ever considered. Her father was no different from her uncles or friends' fathers. Like most men of his generation, his focus was on providing financially for his family. As an insurance salesman he'd spent most of his time with clients, cold calling, or participating in Rotary Club to help increase his client pool and grow his agency. Taking issue with his confession, she reminded him how he had come into her room every night and talked to her before she went to sleep. And he had been very "liberated" when it came to her participation in activities that were considered more typical for males—lawn mowing, baseball, carpentry, and attending law school. She told him how she always felt safe and loved, and how proud she was whenever she glimpsed something of him in herself—her sense of humor, appreciation of nature, and remaining true to her values. Writing the letter was a rare moment when she did not censor her emotions. As soon as the envelope slid down the slot of the mailbox, she wanted to grab it back. Her family, particularly her Dad, avoided sentimentality, and she was uneasy about the contents of her letter. Her father never mentioned it, and she just assumed, with relief, it had gotten lost in the mail. Now she hoped the post office had delivered it.

Four weeks had passed since she'd seen Heather. Her friend's buying trip to Europe had interfered with their usual bi-monthly dinner dates. When Amelia arrived at the restaurant, Heather greeted her with a kiss on both cheeks.

"I see you've brought a bit of Paris culture back with you."

"Mais oui."

Amelia sniffed the air. "You splurged on La Vie Est Belle perfume!"

"A gift from a designer."

"Lucky you."

The waiter asked if they wanted something to drink. Heather chose a dry martini with a twist of lemon, and Amelia decided on a glass of Chardonnay. Recently, she'd concluded Heather ordered a martini because it projected a sophisticated image. She never finished it and when dinner was served would switch to wine.

"So, how was your trip?"

Heather smiled. "It was a very pleasant break. Everyone was so well-mannered, and from a business standpoint, it was very successful. What about you? Any news from the home front?"

Amelia couldn't figure out how to start from the beginning, so she began at a later point. "The man I saw who appeared to look like my father, his name is Arthur Stevenson. I read to him four days a week."

Heather, about to swallow a sip of her drink, choked. "You're reading to your father's doppelganger! How did that happen?"

"Really, Heather? Doppelgangers are a myth. Studies have shown people who claim they've seen a carbon copy either aren't well acquainted with the comparison person or haven't had time to study the look-alike."

"Are you avoiding my question? Tell me everything from the very first day."

Heather's request kicked Amelia back into the morass of her obsessive thoughts and odd actions. But perhaps if she told her story out loud, she could sort through her confusion. Amelia got through the explanation of how she'd stolen into Arthur's apartment building and seen the notice. When she reached the description of their first meeting, her pursuit of a man she'd glimpsed through her window left her perplexed as to her motives. Had she hoped to find someone who was a facsimile of her father?

"When I met Arthur, I saw that any resemblance to my father was a trick of lighting and distance. Other than baldness and perhaps the shape of his mouth, there is no physical similarity. I would guess he's around eighty-three, the same age my father would be had he lived, and he sounds much the same as my Dad; his choice of words, his references, but that may be generational. It's as if he's a person from my past, an old friend of my parents or a childhood neighbor."

What Amelia said to Heather was accurate but didn't describe how emotional the encounter had been for her.

"Well, that's nice. But why are you doing this?"

Amelia looked down at her hands as if she would find the answer written on her palm. "I don't know why. Do you think I'm being really weird?"

"Weird is our window dresser, Jordan, who's convinced he's the reincarnation of Cleopatra's cat. A cat, for Christ's sake! What's that?! Although, he has the 'no matter what you say I'll do what I want to do so screw you' personality of a cat."

Amelia wondered if Heather was just trying to placate her, but her expression was difficult to read.

"So, as long as I'm compared to Jordan, my behavior will seem perfectly normal?" Amelia couldn't help but laugh, which washed away her concerns. Then the conversational spotlight turned back upon Heather, and she didn't have to deal with the subject for the rest of the evening.

Amelia read to Arthur for two more months. She looked forward to their time together. It gave her the chance to share a book she loved with an appreciative audience, and as the days went by, they also took more frequent breaks to chat. After their first meeting, they never touched on their personal lives. Any mention of background or family was superficial and secondary to what they were discussing. Of course, they talked about Rostov, the protagonist of the book, and the beautifully fleshed out supporting characters who inhabited Rostov's new world. After she'd read a few chapters, Arthur grumbled that Rostov appeared not to appreciate the fact that his imprisonment did not include solitary confinement. It started Amelia wondering about how much time Arthur spent by himself. Her father was lucky to have plenty of visitors when he was sick. Her parents' circle of friends included people they'd known in Connecticut who had also retired in or around Naples, and long-time neighbors in their complex. One of her father's brothers and his wife also lived about thirty minutes away. She hoped she was not the only one to visit Arthur. She couldn't know for sure without asking, but the question seemed too personal.

Sometimes Amelia and Arthur discussed subjects removed from the topic of the book. He said he enjoyed learning about what the younger generation was thinking and doing in a world increasingly foreign to him. When she mentioned a special exhibition of Impressionists at the Metropolitan she planned on viewing, they found they had a common love of those painters, in particular, Monet, Cezanne and Degas. Amelia told him she'd wouldn't have been familiar with artists and their work if her father hadn't insisted she take an Art Appreciation course her freshman year of college. She was still grateful her father had been so adamant.

She'd never known her father was particularly interested in art, although once or twice during her childhood, her parents dragged her around an art museum. When she associated her Dad with painting, it conjured an image of the familiar planes of his face spattered with her favorite shade of blue. He had spent a Sunday afternoon rolling the color on her bedroom walls after she'd told him she was too old for pink wallpaper with rainbows and purple butterflies.

For two days in the beginning of March, the temperature rose into the high 50's. At lunchtime, coatless people congregated in the streets, and tee-shirted young men on rollerblades and Razor scooters, wove a path between pedestrians, their young bodies on public view for the first time in months. All around her, people exuded a celebratory mood, the weariness of winter put aside and the hope for an early spring palpable.

On the first day of the warm spell, she arrived at Arthur's apartment to find the windows partially opened and an elaborate tea with blueberry scones and lemon pound cake laid out for the two of them.

"What's all this?"

Arthur's cheeks were pink and his grin wide, "I thought we'd have a treat today to usher in Spring."

"You don't suppose it's just a temporary thaw?"

"I've decided to be optimistic."

Amelia wondered if it was more than the weather. Maybe he'd gotten some good news. For a little while her heart lifted. Two days later, a bitter cold wind blew snow through the canyons of the city where it collected in dirty piles in the gutters. Maybe it was a warning that you should never expect too much.

She didn't talk about her friendship with Arthur or her growing unease with anyone but Heather.

It was the kind of story she would have shared with her father if he were alive. From childhood, she had trusted him with her secrets, like the time she was eleven and had whispered in his ear, "I love Joey Benton and he says he loves me."

He had nodded and pantomimed locking his lips and throwing away the key.

At the end of April, the bony scaffolding of Arthur's face and hands became more prominent, and he appeared to have some discomfort. He often shifted his position in his chair and added a pillow behind his back. He also chatted less, letting her read most of the time, and ended their sessions earlier. One Monday morning, she got a call from Arthur's caregiver. He told her Arthur needed to discontinue their visits but wanted her to stop by at noon on Friday for a few minutes.

Amelia's hand shook as she hung up the phone. A shiver ran through her. Now, it was impossible for her to deny what she had suspected from the beginning. Arthur was dying and soon there would be one more void in her life nobody else could fill. Amelia wanted to give him a parting gift, but what do you get for a man who no longer needed possessions. Before catching her commuter train, she walked four blocks in the opposite direction to a stationery store, where she bought a box of paper and envelopes made from heavy cream-colored stock, a Waterman fountain pen, and a package of black ink cartridges. Once home, Amelia retreated to the quiet of her bedroom. In meticulous script, she wrote a well-thought-out thank you, which attempted to convey the immense enjoyment and comfort reading to him had brought her. She ended by telling him, "In the brief time we've spent together, as with the best of artists, you have enlarged my world." Eyes wet, she signed the note, "With deep affection."

On Friday, the walk to Arthur's place went by much too fast. If she searched an entire unabridged dictionary, she would not find the right words to mark the end of their time together.

When she arrived at the apartment, his caregiver let her in and stood with her in the foyer.

Amelia looked into the living room, but her friend was not there.

"Arthur asked me to apologize for him. He planned to say goodbye in person, but he isn't up to it. He told me to give you this," the nurse said. He handed Amelia a small narrow box wrapped in elegant gold paper and tied with a ribbon of deep pink satin.

Amelia thanked him and gave him her note for Arthur. "Please tell him goodbye for me," she said as a film of tears fought to the surface of her eyes despite her best effort to contain them. After the door closed behind her, she stood there for a moment to compose herself before she left the building.

In the privacy of her office, Amelia unwrapped her present. She had hoped there would be a card in the box, but when she opened the lid, all she saw was a layer of pink tissue paper. Underneath it, she found a black velvet pouch. Inside was Arthur's first acquisition to his antique bookmark collection. The sword's silver blade gleamed in the light, and the intricate gothic carving on the hilt amazed her. She placed it in the palm of her hand and stroked the miniature masterpiece with her finger. It was then she understood how superfluous a note from Arthur would have been. His choice of a gift spoke more eloquently than her note.

As Amelia gazed at the sword, she felt sad that her time with Arthur had been so brief, and grateful she'd been allowed her father's company for the most important moments in her life: her graduations, her wedding, and the birth of her children. The memory of her first child's birth surfaced and she was transported back in time. There was her Dad beside her, his arms swaddling his grandson. For a few moments, he stared down at the newborn, and then he looked up and fixed his attention on Amelia, as if he was a compass needle and she was true north. This mental picture made her smile for the first time in days.

The next evening, Amelia lay propped up in bed with her copy of *A Gentleman in Moscow* face down in her lap. Earlier in the day, she'd remembered the box of her father's important papers, still stored in the back of a coat closet at her mother's home in Florida. Amelia considered whether she should visit her. It was possible the letter she'd sent to her Dad so many years ago was among his possessions, providing proof it had been received and read. She pushed her speculation aside for the moment and turned her book over. For the past few months, she had spoken the words aloud and forgotten what it was like to read silently. And it came to her, both methods revealed what the author wanted to convey. Her body softened with contentment. How foolish it was to worry about whether her Dad had received her letter – she had the answer she'd been searching for. Fingering her new bookmark, Amelia decided she'd keep it on her bedside table within arms-reach, in case she needed to mark her place.

Motherhood on 11x17 Canvas, Mixed Media
3rd Place in the Derick Burleson Poetry Contest

Victoria James

I'm a cool palate, blue, purple, green -
I wish - reality, I'm warm: spicy red, sour yellow, sticky orange -
the colors of candy nobody likes.

Throw me on a Canvas every which way:
Palette knife me down, smear my edges to keep
me in place. Water me down to spread me thinner
to use me more than I'm meant for.

Blood red blends with velvet cream.
Bag up the .5oz of strawberry milk glaze,
throw it, sculpt it, burn it in the kiln.
Title the sculpture, Failed Attempt at Breastfeeding.

Mix me with alcohol ink and watch me
swing hazy, dance lazy, and think crazy
all over the paper, forgetting every direction.

Step back, look at the masterpiece:
She's a little dysfunctional, a little messy,
a mixed media piece of sorts, but damn
what a picture she's made. An artist.

Silhouettes on a Country Road
Finalist in the Mary Cassatt Art Contest

Karen Colstrom

The Headmaster
3rd place in the Ben Nyberg Fiction Contest

Greta Holt

"What the hell did I say now?" Jason Stevens raked a hand through his hair. "All I asked for was corn."

He joined Hans Gerber lounging outside the store by the bikes.

Hans lifted his eyes heavenward and sighed. "How did you say it?"

I said, "Do you have any good *mabele?*"

Hans kicked his bike stand up. "Let's go. You just asked a Motswana woman if she has good breasts."

'Aw, shit." Stevens slung his grocery bags into the basket. He hauled out his Setswana dictionary from his pocket. "No. See, *mabele* means corn—and breasts. Damn. I still can't keep the tones straight."

Hans struck a tragic pose. "I just know you asked for it over and over." He started pedaling. "Come on."

"Wait." Stevens turned toward the store window. With his hands together as in prayer, he pantomimed, 'I'm sorry! 'He pointed to the dictionary. Then he slapped his forehead. He knew the women were watching and laughing softly behind their hands.

"It's good you have a wife," Hans shouted back at him. Some townsmen waved vaguely, their attention on attaching a donkey in harness to the back end of a cut-in-half Citroen. Stevens aimed a grin at the store and followed Hans.

Hans clicked his tongue like an old schoolmarm. "The Headmaster of a school, and a man your age."

"Funny, damn funny." Where would Dr. Jason Stevens be without his charm? He wondered if there would be a time he would run out of patience at being laughed at.

The two men biked up the small incline toward the school. Jason Stevens, Headmaster of Delta Secondary School, wanted to get back to work. It had been a good morning at the village *kgotla*. Under the thatched roof in the open air tribal court, he'd blocked a plan to set up a bottle store near the school, and he'd talked the council into letting him start building four new classrooms.

Delta Secondary and the surrounding town separated the lush Okavango Delta from the expanse of the Kalahari Desert. The day was cloudless and warm. Playful swirls of wind lifted the sand between a few cinder block stores. The men waved to the zebra herd behind the fence at the Ngamiland Game Study Reserve. As usual, the zebra turned away but gazed over their shoulders like coy beauty queens.

"Like women," Stevens said.

"Ya-ah," said Hans.

The Batswana women were beautiful, with high cheekbones and willowy waists, and their British-tribal accent impressed the hell out of his American heart. Stevens found himself wanting to drape an arm around them, in a friendly way.

Stevens and Hans dodged a family of goats and swerved around the new, lopsided sign outside Mma Toise's rondavel that read,' Business and Professional Women's Club of Botswana. 'A big name for only the second such club in the country, Stevens thought. Its membership was just a few teachers and nurses.

"Ann joined right away." He pedaled easily.

"Ah, your wife is..." Hans puffed through the heavier sand at the side of the road, "...your best asset."

"Yeah." Ann had started to tell him something last night about the latest meeting of the women's club, but he'd fallen asleep. A Headmaster was live-in principal, counselor, and maintenance man, stirred into a dizzying concoction including international host and tour guide. Sometimes he and Ann would escape to Safari House on the tourist side of the village; alone, they could sink into malt Scotch, and he could whine until he got tired of it, or she did.

"You know." Stevens voice was dreamy. "I'm going to take a picture of those zebra, and when Mannheim makes up another excuse to get out of evening study supervision, I'll just whip out my picture and give him a load of zebra butt. And you'll notice I said zebra with a short e and no 's', and it's football, not soccer. And petrol, not gas. And you give a guy a leeft, not a lift." He glanced with satisfaction at the gate's yellow and blue portrait of an elephant frolicking in the Thamalakane River. He'd flattered the best art student.

Hans sighed. "You're good with us, Jason." He stood on the pedals and coasted. "Our Cambridge scores could beat Gaborone's."

"Not good enough." Stevens sped the last sixty yards to the newly painted school gate with its thatched roof.

"With all due respect, you've only been here a few months." Hans, winded, pulled up beside him. "Even though I hasten to say, *meinleader*, you are doing a fine job."

Stevens jumped off his bike and walked it toward his house. "I was looking in the attendance files yesterday. You know the girls 'dropout rate is much higher than the boys'. Why's that?"

Hans laughed shortly. "Talk to Mrs. Pilane, she..."

They saw them coming across campus. Boys, fists pumping, chanting, and yelling.

"Damn," said Hans. "Honeymoon's over. Welcome to Africa."

"What do they want?"

"Look, there's Kaunga in tow, trying to stop them."

Stevens gazed at the forty-some boys shouting and marching across the soccer field toward the teachers 'quarters. "Take my bike."

He strode to his Jeep, jumped behind the wheel, and turned the key. This is what he'd been waiting for. Despite his complaining, things had been too nice, people overly responsive. 'Oh, Dr. Stevens, we're so happy you're here. The school was just in shambles before you came. '
Get real.

But this was his meat and potatoes. *Come on, baby-faced boys. Meet an American principal. Let's see what you got.*

Dr. Jason Stevens jerked the gears and turned the Jeep toward the crowd. He revved the engine, then drove straight toward them.

At the sight of the big American in the noisy Jeep, the weaker-willed boys split from the group like ants run amuck. By the time Stevens jerked to a halt in front of the boys, only about twenty were left. So much for teenaged bravado.

The Headboy, Kaunga, pushed to the front. "Dr. Stevens, sir. I am sorry. I tried to stop them, but it is as you can see."

A soccer player stepped up. "Keep quiet, Kaunga. We can speak; we have the right. We do not need the Headboy to present our case."

All six feet four inches of Stevens stood. He took his time for effect, one foot on top of the Jeep's window casing and the other on the rim between the front seats. He ignored the soccer student.

"Listen up." His voice splintered the sunshine. "In America, I've dealt with students who shouted they had rights. By that, they meant they had something worthy to say." Stevens shrugged, almost to himself. "Rarely did."

He planted his hands on his hips. "But you. You are the elite. To come to this school, you've passed tests that would send American students screaming into the bush. I expect what you have to say is worthy of hearing. But—and get this straight, gentlemen—I don't talk to mobs, and I won't start now. If what you have to say is important, you'll pick a leader from each Form. The leaders will come with well-written notes to my house. They'll meet with me in the home of my wife and my child." He was aware of playing that card. "They will sit and present their arguments in a formal manner. I will be honest in my responses."

He dropped back onto the seat in one fluid motion, revved the Jeep's engine and turned the vehicle as if to go. "And one more thing, boys." He nailed them. "Don't ever approach me with your 'rights' if the word 'responsibilities' doesn't come out of your mouths in the same sentence. Seven o'clock tonight at my house." He left them standing on the field, eating dust from his tires. They hadn't been able to stammer, shout, or speak one complaint.

Jason Stevens laughed out loud. Kids. Everywhere the same: suckers for a little good leadership. He didn't understand weak educators; he never had. The fight was worth it and the alternatives too horrible to live with. If this was all they could throw at him, things were going to be even better than in the States. His next malt Scotch would be a victory toast. Jason down-shifted hard.

He turned off the engine. Jesus, he loved it. "Botswana! Rather spectacular, I say, old chap, whot?"

"What? How did it go?" Hans had been waiting in his adjoining yard with the gate closed.

"No sweat." Stevens grinned at Hans's face and bounded up his walk. He opened the door and swung his wife off the ground.

"Are you okay?" Ann gasped in mid-air.

"We're in! First salvos fired, and the war's already over." He danced her around little Bobby's high chair.

"But Hans said it looked bad."

"Hans plays with numbers, dear. He's not," taking a step, "in," dancing a second step, "charge!" He ended with a low dip and swung her up into a hug.

Ann kissed him. "Okay, okay." Her eyebrow rose. "So you're the best in Botswana." She took his face in her hands. "Just remember, it's their country."

"Yeah, but it's my school."

After supper, Stevens spent a few minutes with his Setswana phrasebook. Yesterday, Ann told him about a student's translation of the ark passage: "...and Noah, he transported carnivorous and herbivorous animals to the ark." These kids grew up speaking their own tribal languages, then learned Setswana, and finally tackled English. If they could live inside their dictionaries, he could, too. Stevens would not allow himself to be the one-language American.

Since coming here, Jason surprised himself with the sudden formality of his speech. Hell, he sounded like that kid in junior high who got stuffed into the ball bin.

Promptly at 7:00 PM, apparently out of respect for European time, the chosen boys knocked at the door. They had dressed to regulation in blue trousers, white shirts, and thin blue ties. There were four, one each for Forms III, IV, and V, plus the Headboy, Kaunga. Stevens was amused to see not only were the younger students not represented, but the soccer kid had not been chosen. The boys must have decided this was serious work.

"*Dumela*, Dr. Stevens, sir."

"*Dumelang*, students." He ushered them inside. "*Gaetsho ke fa. Mosadi wa me. Ke ngwanake.*" He made a sweeping gesture of his house, his wife, his child.

Each student solemnly shook hands with his wife who had been drafted as a Bible Knowledge teacher. Victor Moruti and Kaunga chucked little Bobby under his chin and ruffled his hair. Bobby favored them with his newest dance, which consisted of bouncing up and down and piercing the air with screams. Formalities over, the boys and the Headmaster sat on leopard-spot vinyl chairs in the living room. Ann served coffee and cookies. The boys opened their notes and readied their pens.

"Dr. Stevens, sir, thank you and Mma Stevens for this supper. We have not eaten the school meal out of protest today." As the school's newspaper editor, Victor Moruti held the most powerful position on campus. The others nodded solemnly. "The problem is most students would rather make their own fat cakes than endure the poor quality of the meali-meal Mr. Jake serves us."

Did they ever use a contraction? Was this about the food?

"If I may speak, please," said Bareetsi Nyunyu, the school's best debater. "The porridge does not contain margarine, but we believe Mr. Jake has received a shipment from Francistown two days ago. It is suspect he uses this butter for his own family, rather than in our meals."

"And the Prefects!" interrupted Matthew Ribane, the youngest representative. "They tell the Boardingmaster when we go the Chibuku depot because of hunger, and then something macabre will happen to us." The others stared at him in something like horror.

Jason Stevens wanted to hug Matthew Ribane. He didn't dare look at Ann as he said, "Mma Stevens, get our own notebook and write, please. All right, boys. Macabre things happen to you when you go to a Chibuku depot, and the Prefects tell on you? Explain."

"We..."

Victor Moruti cut off Matthew. "Dr. Stevens, sir, Chibuku is a kind of beer. So a Chibuku depot is a bottle store, as you know. It is two kilometers away, and to go there is against the rules, as it is off campus."

He knew that.

Ann wrote busily.

"The students who go," Victor continued, "know they are committing a sin against the school rules, but most do not ever go there for the drink." He threw Matthew a sharp look. "They only want to combine a few *thebe* and eat a good meal. This is wrong, but the anger comes at the Prefects for speaking ill of us but not attempting to fix this problem of the food."

"Yes!" Matthew broke in again. "And the Prefects, especially the Headboy, think they are the Headmaster. They tell us to eat poorly-cooked beans, when none of the students wish to eat them, and…"

Victor glared at Matthew.

Stevens leaned back. Fancy English, kids' minds. "First, where is your proof none of the students are eating beans? And second, where is your proof Mr. Jake has taken the butter?"

The boys spoke at once. The evidence consisted of asking around, and somebody saying something to someone, who gossiped to someone else, who was sure it had happened.

Then the boys were finished.

"Your evidence is not good, gentlemen." Stevens almost clucked his tongue. "And yet, I might address these things with you if…"

"But then, please sir, there is our study time," Bareetsi, the debater, interrupted, "in which the Headboy pretends he is a teacher and makes strong references to our study habits." He flourished his notes in Kaunga's direction. "Many feel the Prefects and the Headboy are corrupted by their power."

Young Matthew Ribane nodded vigorously and munched his peanut butter cookie.

The Headboy Kaunga stood. He was as tall as Headmaster Stevens.

"Sir, from the moment I decided upon a path of education, I have known I would go on to university. Perhaps this is why I have been chosen as leader." The young man turned to the boys. "I have heard you murmur names against me as I go by. Often you have said threats of dunking me in the river or covering me with pig dung."

Kaunga nodded at Ann. "Since I have learned your religion, Madame, I have known there is right and wrong, not just what each of us wants at a moment." He spoke to the boys. "Wherever there are groups living together, there must be some rules. When rules exist, they must be obeyed. That is my responsibility, which I accept. Now, do you think I'm going to stop doing right because you are threatening me? No!"

"You state your position well, Kaunga." Stevens noted the boy had crossed his arms on his chest, a stance resembling his own. "Now, I will state mine. Gentlemen, first the issue of meals. Write this down, please, Mma.

Jason Stevens, Headmaster, outlined a plan in which he himself would eat with the students for a week. Then he would invite Mr. Jake to face the boys. All parties would have their say. At this, Matthew Ribane dropped his forehead into his hand.

Stevens reminded the boys of their own democratic precepts of facing one's accusers and being innocent until proven guilty. Then he admonished them to tell all the students any of them found at the Chibuku depot would be sent home, without appeal.

"But what about the Prefects?" Matthew seemed to try not to whine.

"A debate!" Bareetsi jumped up. "We must have a school debate on this issue."

Victor and Kaunga readily agreed. "It would be the fairest course."

In the end, it was decided the debate would be held on Friday before the day-students went home. The regular debate team would be changed to afford those who held opposite opinions a chance to present the arguments dearest to their hearts. Those in favor of the present system of student government would be represented by Victor Moruti, Robert of the debate team, and Kaunga. Those presenting arguments against would be Bareetsi, Matthew Ribane, and Ntikina of the agriculture club.

The boys left, still arguing. They carried a tin of Ann's almond raisin cookies and a couple pints of milk.

"Well, that was ballsy," laughed Stevens. "Kaunga's got guts, and that Victor has a level head."

"Such an assembly of masculinity." Ann began to clean up. "You were just wonderful."

Jason was never quite sure if his wife was serious, especially about him. That raised right eyebrow of hers tended to bring on ironic comments. He looked at her; there it was, floating toward her hairline. He held his breath.

"Jason, what about the girls? Shouldn't they be represented in the debate?"

"Oh, god, yes. Listen, I'll take care of it tomorrow. I'll see Mrs. Pilane, that Motswana English teacher. She's a lousy disciplinarian, but she knows the girls. Isn't there a really good student, Delilah somebody, who's supposed to ace the Cambridge in November? Hans says she has the highest female average ever in math—maths, whatever. Why didn't you remind me to include the girls?"

"I..." Ann moved the dishrag around a plate slowly. "You know, we need to talk soon about something Mrs. Pilane said last week at the professional women's..."

"Aw, crap. Now I have to change the calendar, and we just finished it. And I've got to talk to that jerk, Mr. Jake. Probably is stealing the butter." He stretched and moved in on his wife. "Let's go to bed, Mma." Stevens ducked the damp dishrag and threw it back. They tried not to wake up the baby as they tussled among the rooms of the little house.

The next morning, Headmaster Stevens mediated an argument between Swedish and Zambian teachers about which one was taking the other's South African #2 pencils, until the Swede remembered he'd lent them to a pretty Namibian teacher in hopes of a little company on a trip down to Ghanzi. Stevens organized a clean-up detail for the big toilet houses, or 'absolution blocks.' When he tried to make a call to the Ministry of Education in Gaborone, the phones were down for the third time this week.

On the way to see Mrs. Pilane, he was waylaid by a Form IV government teacher complaining about a student who had skipped class to go fishing in the river behind the school farm. Stevens wrote a punishment detail that would have the student chopping out tree stumps from 1:00 to 3:00 on Saturday afternoon.

Crossing the soccer field to his house on the riverbank, Stevens caught shouts of greeting. He kept turning, starting to wave, but finding no one. Conversations in the village—acoustic aberrations—floated across the river and echoed on the school grounds. After four months here, he was still fooled.

He stopped briefly to look at the turnip and kale shoots which, when the rains came, would be added to the school's menu. The predictions were good, and the river flowed. The school was rapidly becoming a showcase for sustainable farming. They'd make a name for themselves with the agriculture, and then hit 'em with their Cambridge scores. Stevens smiled.

The warmth of the day was turning rapidly to heat, and the odor of shredded beef on village cooking fires settled over the campus like an oily mist. A line of sweat ran down Jason's temple. It was going to get hot. He wished he had remembered one of his baseball caps.

Mrs. Pilane's blockhouse was situated under the acacia trees. Stevens admired the new white and blue paint on its door. Soon, he'd have students paint murals on the front of each classroom.

Bowing to the afternoon's rising temperature, Mrs. Pilane had positioned her class outside on the half-moon seats in the shade. She was trying to explain prepositions, as his new, Americanized curriculum demanded, and no one was listening. He watched her: delicate hands, graceful hips. As the students became aware of him leaning against a tree behind them, even the boys straightened their backs and pretended to write busily in their notebooks. Dr. Stevens's reputation preceded him.

Mrs. Pilane's voice was weak and her delivery muddled. She turned her back on the class to write each preposition on the board. Stevens found himself biting his knuckles as she droned on. Sweat started under his arms.

"Mrs. Pilane, may I?" It was said before he could stop himself.

Startled, she wiped a streak of yellow chalk first on her forehead, then down the front of her dress. "Oh, of course, Headmaster Stevens."

He strode to the front. She looked so anxious his arm reached out to her, but he caught himself and ran his hand through his hair instead. "Students, Mrs. Pilane is giving you an important list. Write it." They wrote, and he moved among them correcting and encouraging. He was back in front of the class in two steps.

"Now, with Mrs. Pilane's permission, I am going to show you how to Remember This List and Like It!" The students giggled. In an exaggerated rhythm, he chanted a rhyme, gestured to them, and they began to repeat the rhyme, substituting new prepositions. They laughed and clapped as each successive word made a different word picture.

"Now I have a challenge for you. Each of you will make a picture that corresponds to one of the prepositional phrases. Yes, you may make pictures in your notebooks."

He took the hand of a serious-looking student and led her to the front. "What is your name? Miriam? Miriam will assign a phrase to each of you. Draw carefully, students, raise your hands, and work well while I talk with Mrs. Pilane about another matter." He watched a moment to be sure the girl he had picked was exercising her authority with relish. Then he turned to Mrs. Pilane.

She had retreated to the side of the blackboard. He took her arm and guided her a few steps away into the off-concrete sand. "Thank you, Mrs. Pilane. Maybe I miss teaching a bit?" He cocked his head and grinned down at her. "You were doing a fine job."

"Headmaster, it is a pleasure to have you demonstrate for us." Mrs. Pilane's back was straight and her gaze fell somewhere between his cheek and chin.

"Well, that's not the reason I've come. I need to talk to some of the good students about a debate Friday, and I'd like you to see that some of the older girls take part. Ann says Delilah—uh, that math student?"

"Delilah Masedi, sir."

"She said the girl is an excellent student. Perhaps you could recommend a few more?"

"Oh, but Dr. Stevens, Delilah is presently in your office. She is withdrawing today."

"What?"

Mrs. Pilane moved a few more steps from the class and lowered her voice. "She has responsibilities."

"What responsibilities? This is a very good student. I'm sure we can help. Is it the school fees?"

"No, Dr. Stevens. Many of the girls who are day students take care of the young ones at home by themselves. Parents are often at the cattle station or the crop lands. The older girls take care of everything: cooking, cleaning, washing clothes. It is much work." Mrs. Pilane smoothed her skirt. "And, for some, if they are, called out…"

"Stay with it!" Stevens had turned to keep the students on task. "Mrs. Pilane, perhaps you and my wife could conference about some ways to keep the students involved. What were you saying about Delilah?"

Mrs. Pilane narrowed her eyes and stared past his left shoulder a moment, then seemed to make a decision. She began to walk past him toward her class.

"Mrs. Pilane." His voice stopped her.

Mrs. Pilane turned. "She is satisfied," she said softly, and walked to the front of her class.

"Satisfied?" Stevens was stunned. "Satisfied?" A warning nipped at him. "We cannot have good students deciding they've had enough." He snagged his sock on a thorny bush as he followed, irritated that he was abruptly in front of the class. "Mrs. Pilane, I know you, as an educated woman, support the continuing education of our girls."

The students were staring at him. Suddenly, holding back for just a split second, or at least lowering his voice, seemed awfully important, but he plowed ahead. He gestured at the girls, most of whom filled the first two rows.

"Young ladies, you must not be satisfied with less than a full education. Many of you will eventually earn a first or second pass on the Cambridge, and you will find yourselves at university, taking your place among the brightest of Botswana. I'm sure Mrs. Pilane agrees you must not be satisfied until you achieve your dreams."

The students sat. Some looked at their knees, a few glanced at each other, while others sat bolt upright and seemed to gaze behind Stevens at the orange trees on the edge of the school farm. One or two of them stared outright at him, as did Mrs. Pilane. A few students hiccuped behind their hands.

Stevens felt the sun hammer his moist neck. A thin odor from the absolution blocks seeped into the enclosure. "Well, uh, let's see the pictures you have made."

"We are still working, Headmaster," said the leader, Miriam.

He tossed the chalk he'd been clutching into the chalkwell. "Good. So. Mrs. Pilane, thank you for allowing me to visit your fine class. Work well, students, and listen to Mma Pilane."

Retreating down the gravel path he thought he heard giggling, but it was quickly stifled.

The dismissal bell rang. Sweat pricked Stevens's scalp. A large globule fell down his neck as he strode into the soccer field's clearing—*football* field, his mind corrected. He was annoyed. Mrs. Pilane's response had been terse, and he had lost the class. He hated not knowing why, but his years of experience were letting him guess. He glanced up to see two tiny dirt tornados destroy each other in a fleeting dance over the river.

"Have you noticed how we all huddle under the trees like cattle when it becomes hot?"

"Afternoon, Hans."

They stopped under a mopani tree by the field where the Delta Gold Tigers were practicing for next month's game with Francistown. Seth Harleman, the banned South African center mid, was running drills. Matthew Ribane and Duke waved. Across the field under a large shade tree, they saw Kaunga, Bareetsi, and Victor Moruti with notebooks, probably conferring about tomorrow's debate.

"Delilah Masedi is in your office."

"Hans, what do I do about this?"

Hans draped his arms over a branch. "She has to go. The Board of Trustees will insist."

"Why?"

"She's pregnant."

" Ah, shit." Stevens sighed. "Who's responsible?"

"That, Herr Headmaster, will not be an issue."

"The hell it won't. If one of our girls is dismissed, the boy who did it is out."

Students began filling the area around the field. They called to friends and strolled past in small groups. It irritated Stevens that he did not know most of their names.

"Jason, listen. You're a good Headmaster, we need you. And none of us can say that easily."

"Well, that's nice, but…"

"Just listen to me. I've been here six years." Hans pulled his tie loose. "The Batswana are smart. They took what they wanted from the British and kept their own laws. But you must understand something; it's essential, my friend."

They watched a group of JC girls walk toward the cafeteria. The skirts of their school uniforms floated around their thighs in the afternoon heat. Stevens felt dizzy at the thought of a long, cool bath.

Hans continued, "There will be no search for the male who made Delilah Masedi pregnant. Most of the time, if a girl is 'called out' by a boy, she goes. It's mixed up with pride, fertility, duty maybe."

"Look, I don't need a lecture on…"

"It's accepted, yet it's not. Sometimes the men stay around; sometimes they don't. I've heard some Batswana blame the British, an easy target, and others actually blame the decline of polygamy for it! Hell, I don't know."

"Wait, wait."

"There's more." Hans stared at the players practicing headers. "Hints about girls being, well, hurt if they refuse."

Seth Harleman shouted furiously at a forward as the boys sped by.

"Not here. Not on my campus."

"I don't know; it probably just happens in the village. You hear things. But, in all my years here, only three rape cases have ever been tried. One had a conviction, and the man was fined twelve *pula* or three days in jail. Mrs. Pilane told me she brought up the problem to that new professional women's group last week. You know, that sign we passed yesterday."

Stevens felt perspiration spread over his chest. "Doesn't the church care about finding the father?"

"Come on, the mission board made you sit through training, too. What's more important to people: their religion or their habits?" Hans poked at the dirt with a sandled toe. "Look at these boys. Maybe one of them called out Delilah Masedi. Maybe it was an older man from town. And maybe…" Hans kicked down at the dirt so high it flew. "You hear, with teachers moving around so much. I mean, you hear about teachers."

Jason Stevens groaned.

"But she went." Hans said. "Delilah was called out, and she went. Now, it's she who leaves. That's the way it is."

"But we've got to do something about it!"

"You've already forgotten the women's group?" He dropped a heavy hand on Stevens's shoulder. "Okay, Headmaster, take on every issue yourself; take it all on, burn out, and transfer to the Ministry of Education in 'Gabs 'next year, like the others do. You'll feel righteous."

"Dammit, Hans." He shook him off. "I can't just let it go. The girl's knocked up. She had a future." Across the field, Kaunga the Headboy stood and made a sweeping gesture as Victor wrote in his notebook. "Kaunga will help me. I'll ask him to find out who did it."

Hans turned to go. "You've never heard of perks?"

Stevens sat down under the tree. He watched a dirt devil attack the little grey and white rondavel chapel building, scattering the short-tailed cats nesting in its thatched roof. The heat shimmered now, foreshadowing savage summer winds from Namibia. Ancient storms had spit the delta's thin soil onto the Kalahari Desert.

He remembered how the dust had kicked up outside the half-roofed pink church in the village the day they'd arrived. One minute he'd been greeting the minister and his wife, both refugees from Angola. They were telling him about the times they had been put in front of firing squads as they tried to get out. The next minute, he couldn't see them for the sand whipping about. He'd shielded his eyes and tried to make out the church and the people through the coarse, copper fog. But for that moment, all of them were gone.

What was it about going so far from home that made a person feel like an idiot, or more exactly, a babe in arms? Events seemed veiled in shadows, and he couldn't make out the corners. His mind squinted, and the obvious escaped him.

What had Mrs. Pilane said? 'She is satisfied.' Stevens swiped at his neck with the tail of his shirt and took out his dictionary. He looked for definitions of 'pregnant.' Yeah, he got it; he got it.

'Pregnant , adj. Become pregnant'- *ithwala.* 'She is pregnant '–*o ithwele.*

'Become pregnant, of cattle '–*nemeruhala.*

Stevens almost threw the book.

Then he saw, 'Pregnant of an illegitimate child '–*ithwala mpa ea dikgora.*

He looked up each word. *Ithwala*—'conceive.' *Mpa* 'a belly.'

Ea—This one's definition was so long he had to guess... . 'pronoun 3rd person of nouns with no prefix for singular, but whose plural prefix is *di*; It-they.' Jesus Christ.

Dikgora—...'this word is also used to denote illegitimacy, of a child, and illicit intercourse on the part of an adult.'

The definitions for *dikgora* went on, giving the Setswana phrases for 'an illegitimate child, a woman who has illegitimate children, a loose-living woman: a prostitute.' His temples started to throb.

Where was it? He rushed through each definition again. It had to be there... *ithwala* - 'pregnant; '*mpa* - 'belly; '*ea*' whose **plural** prefix is <u>di.</u>'

Shit. *Dikgora—Kgora*! Stevens ripped pages getting to it. *Kgora*--'to be filled; to be fed; to-be-satisfied.'

Jason Stevens, Headmaster, rested his head against the mopani tree. His reputation would precede him, all right. He smiled bleakly. Through half-closed eyes, he watched Kaunga and Victor run toward him, waving their notebooks.

Delilah Masedi was waiting.

The Quiet Body
Finalist in the Derick Burleson Poetry Contest

Dave Malone

Underneath the January snow
lives the garden. This plot is becoming
by sitting still as if reading a book
in wool-socked feet by the fireplace,
with a whiskey in tumbler,
nut brown and warm.

In the fresh snow drift,
I stop garden side
and put elbows to fence
breathing in the silent nature
of this winter quilt,
blocks of last year's basil,
stumps of tomato plants,
stones to mark the rows.

There's a lot happening here
in the quiet body of the garden,
this old lover readying the soil for roots,
for my selfish and greedy hands,
for my fingers full of seed,
for next year's bounty.

Bullfrog Blues
Finalist in the Mary Cassatt Art Contest

Jordyn Elizabeth Plimental

The Supermodels
1st Place in the Phil Heldrich Nonfiction Contest

Jenn Dean

Mid-summer mornings feel heavy, as if the color green has weight. Maples with branches lathered with moss and leaves big as platters overhang the roads. Even the air feels overripe and pliant. Up on the escarpment, the luminous milky plume of Snoqualmie Falls thunders over Tertiary basalt and tuff: an exhalation of rock and air and water. From the road I feel the river pouring over the cliff's granite belly like a liquid thundercloud.

On the upper plateau, I drive past ancient rail cars rusted in place like fossilized sections of a Jurassic python in old town Snoqualmie, then whiz across the prairie, zig-zag through North Bend, and arrive a few minutes later at a dead end: the Olallie State Forest, thirty-eight miles east of Seattle. A trail follows the south fork of the Snoqualmie, and winds through the dense jungled understory. The water shines green and gold. Immense sun-dappled boulders lounge in the middle of the flow like elephants and fly fishermen angle into shallow pools. The sun casts crystals across the wide braided reach, and salmonberry and lacelike vine maple hang thick on the banks. Devils club dangles leaves as big as islands above my head.

The trail winds a mile to the top, where a vertigo-inspiring footbridge spans a two-tiered fall. But it's the woods I've come to see. Uprooted from my native oaks, beeches, and mixed hardwoods of New England, since landing here I've gradually absorbed the flora and fauna, in search of what one novelist calls the 'poetry of survival,' a poetry that feels harder to grasp now that I'm in my sixties. For people even older than myself, the concept of aging-in-place was born, so elders can avoid the indignities of a nursing home. Whether I am bathed or clothed, or worse, drooling, the woods feel like a release from the Psychocene, an era when we attach ourselves to little rectangles in order to witness our own destruction. Today, I'm looking for the ultimate aging-in-placers.

I follow the trail up a steep rise to a bench, where I take in the view from afar. Framed by thick forests, a waterfall sluices down through the evergreens: liquid glass over a two-hundred-foot shale cliff. Below, the river meanders in and out of view, dotted with boulders. Light cascades through the canopy, and plashes of sun light up the chive-green leaves.

A few traverses of the rocky dirt path later, a tree—though that word doesn't aptly describe it—sits down an incline from the path, along a spur that leads to the cobbled shore of the river. If you were hell bent on getting to the falls, you'd miss it, for it grows far enough off the path to obscure its base, big and round as a grain silo. A *Pseudotsuga menziesii,* or Douglas fir. I approach slowly, as one would do an animal, and stare upwards. The bole dives up into the sky. Short branches start fifty feet up, all reaching to one side; on the other side several withered limbs stick out. It appears the crown had been struck by lightning or fell off. If one carved out the base, it would make a suitable four-story dwelling.

Her crenellated bark holds long deep furrows, each giant flake replete with little holes and smaller flakes. Along the bark weave paths of slug slime, and among the crevasses spiders stretch small webs, the bark an apartment complex for who knows how many myriad insects. Beetles heave around the base like guards and ants cross the tree's roots near the bottom as if circumnavigating a mountain; a worn path circles her bole. I place both hands on her skin, then walk slowly around her. On the opposite side, the tree supports a young western hemlock, whose roots start far above my head and look like octopus limbs as they pipe down to the ground. Licorice ferns stick out like green hands, and the bark resembles abraded skin.

I withdraw a long nylon rope from my backpack and let the end rest on the bark at about chest height from the ground, circle the trunk again, then tie the string off and mark it. It measures eighteen feet in circumference, or (divided by π) just under 6 feet in diameter. I multiply the diameter in inches by the growth factor for Douglas fir (5, which means it takes 5 years to put on an inch of girth) which reveals the tree's approximate age: three hundred and sixty years, which makes it older than our unraveling democracy. Taking the Little Ice Age into account, which slowed growth for over three hundred years, I arbitrarily add 140 years to the tree's life, and give it a birthdate of 1520.

I sit with my back up against the bark and open a thermos of caffeine. Not many are aware of this, but one of the largest mining operations in the Pacific Northwest operates in this forest right underneath my derriere. Thousands of workers have painstakingly bored tunnels into the feldspar and hornblende and other rocks in all directions as they search for magnesium, iron, and other minerals. The miners, mischievous daredevils who like to serve up the occasional semi-poisonous meal, don't wear headlamps, or protective gear. They are fungi, uniquely suited to underground conditions. Their fungal threads, or hyphae, extend for miles. Thinner than tapeworms, the hyphae, which merge with the root-hair tips of trees and plants, serve up a slurry of nitrogen, phosphorous, calcium, and potassium. In return, the fungal threads receive a cocktail of carbon and sugar from the tree's root tips. Scientists call this mutualism; non-scientists like myself call it sharing.

The trees work the connections on the fungal map, or mycorrhizal network, like frenzied 1950's stockbrokers on landlines, sending carbon or messages of insect infestations, which signal other trees to turn on their defensive enzymes. Dump carbon! Release the phenolic heteropolymers! A forest is anything but static. If insects or animals get around the structural leaf defenses of wax, thorn, or a leather-like coating, a simple needle chomp by an invader elicits a chemical slurry.

Logging companies, who clear native plants and 'weed trees' like birch, and burn slash, rip the digestive system right out of the forest. They plant seedlings of all the same species, who have no historical networks of mycorrhizas to nourish and protect them. And no mother trees, which have been found to nourish whole colonies of their offspring. Forests empty of old trees, and thus mycorrhizas, are more prone to disease, less healthy, less "productive" as future timber. That we know this is predominantly due to Susan Simard, a sixty-something-year-old British Columbian forester, researcher, and professor, who, like most women in male-dominated arenas, was scoffed at by her male peers and the scientific community throughout the nascent stages of her research, and ridiculed as her published studies, all of which held up to peer review and replication, came to the fore. Her work promulgated the term the "Wood Wide Web," when the gold-standard journal *Nature* published her dissertation findings.[1] Simard suggests that like humans, trees seek connection, diversity, and community. Here the nomenclature gets persnickety—science likes more objective words like "need" over "seek," "mutualism" rather than "share." The big tree at my back—what Simard calls a Mother Tree, old trees with myriad relationships developed over time, trees that feed and nurture the forest as a whole--infuses a body with memory, as if memory were as solid as air, solid as rock. It has a fixity that I envy. And it very much feels like a *who*, not an "it."

If George Vancouver charted the Northwest coast today, he'd find a vastly different landscape than the one he sailed into during his 1791-1795 expedition. When he left the open ocean and coasted into the estuary—the second largest in the country at 95 miles long and five miles wide in some places—he saw, where Seattle's port is today, food-rich tidelands that fanned out from the lower Duwamish (one of many rivers that emptied into the sound). The sound consisted of a huge tidal gash left by the retreat of the ice sheet, pocked with weirdly shaped islands: a tide-filled saltwater wound. On modern maps it appears as if a swimming giant stuck their hand into the land from the Pacific, bent their wrist southward, wiggled their fingers around, then withdrew; the resulting watery shape hooks around the coastal Olympic range, then dives south almost a hundred miles. The largest cities west of the Cascades—Tacoma, Seattle—lie sandwiched between the coast range to the west and the Cascades to the east, and sit starboard on the large multi-fingered waterway we now call the Salish Sea. Pocked with islands, bays, marshes, and underwater canyons, and ringed by volcanoes, the waterway's northern lid—Vancouver Island, BC—he conveniently renamed after himself.

As Vancouver's ship sailed into this protected body of water, from his stance on the quarterdeck he saw dense conifers that furred the land, part of a five-thousand-year-old coastal rainforest that stretched from California to Alaska. Evergreen spires marched all the way down to the watery fringes of the rugged, hilly coastline, and white-mantled volcanoes loomed along the horizon. The trees that furred the coastal expanse included Sitka spruce upwards of 350 feet tall;[2] hemlock and true fir old growth grew in the elevations further inland. Through his spotting scope he saw an endless carpet of vegetable growth on steroids, a site he declared "luxurious."[3] The trees lived 200 to 1,000 years. It was like looking at a giant green pelt.

As he scanned the coastline, contrary to popular imagination, most of the trees he and his crew saw had been growing for only seventy years: a vast inferno, or family of fires, was said to have incinerated[4] the coastal areas in 1701. The flames, which occurred the year after a major megathrust earthquake, may have been intense enough to jump across Colvos Passage, a distance of .9 miles, from the current day Kitsap Peninsula to Vashon Island, as well as hop from shore onto many of the other puzzle-piece islands. The five-hundred-year-long Little Ice Age (1300 to 1850) brought extended drought, severe winter weather, and high wind to the region, all of which created windfalls and deadwood, enough to help ignite a massive scourge of orange and scarlet flames. Three to ten million acres of luxurious green rainforest burned. Although fire scar evidence shows up inland, many of the giants where I live—the Snoqualmie Valley--remained untouched.

The rampaging 1701 burn didn't mean that the trees near the coastline weren't large, they just weren't as large as they would become 150 years later as European settlement began in earnest. Fifty years after Vancouver mapped the area, explorer Charles Wilkes traveled on foot near the Nisqually River area (a river which sources from the southern flank of Mount Rainier and feeds into southern Puget Sound south of Tacoma, which gives an indication of how long the estuary is) and voyaged through a "gigantic fine cedar forest." Wilkes could not contain his astonishment regarding the impenetrable undergrowth between them, nor the way the trees thrust upward like cathedral spires. "Although they are sapplings (sic), [they] are six feet in diameter and upwards of 200 feet in height."[5]

Anywhere from half a billion to a billion trees would have covered the 6,300 square miles that surrounded the Salish Sea up to the lower foothills of the Olympics to the west, and the Cascades to the east. After the fire, which scorched an area more than the size of Denmark, Doug fir would have been one of the first successional trees to take root. Firs, with wood "remarkably fine" as described by Pliny the Roman naturalist, became the future old growth so valuable to the lumberjacks in the late 19th and early 20th centuries.

In 1853, to prepare the newly declared Washington Territory for settlement, the General Land Office began to set imaginary gridlines across the region, their corners marked with posts. Natural trees "witnessed" the grid corners and intersections. The "witness trees," though physically gone today, are recorded in early township archives, and help reveal what forest cover might have looked like even earlier, in pre-Columbian times. Although the average tree measured under nineteen inches, "one of every twenty-six pre-settlement trees was at least four feet across," trees that couldn't be embraced by two people with their arms spread out on either side. Roughly 2,500 to 5,000 of these very large trees grew in each square mile.[6] Some would have been close to three hundred years old; many were located north to south in the watersheds that spill from the Cascade's lip.

Settlers who came to the Snoqualmie Valley from New England, where forests had been depleted, must have felt they had entered a berserk green broccoli forest on growth hormones. A documentary calls this valley Land of the Giants. Situated over a large aquifer, the valley floor held a repository of rich mineral soil spilling out of the mountains, plentiful rain, and a mild climate. The tree trunks swelled to grain-silo size, visions of awe and beauty that produced cravings akin to dreams.

For thousands of years, people all over the world lived in what William Logan Bryant calls "creative engagement" with trees and plants. Bronze Age and Neolithic people pollarded trees in order to grow poles for structures, Mesa Verdeans bent fir trees to get limbs for lintels, and West Africans coppiced trees, which yielded them reliable fence materials to keep animals out, and grain and vegetables free to grow. In Europe, the practice of coppice and pollard had been well known and practiced for centuries, until the land barons came along and wanted pictorial landscapes, not functional ones. Where I live, and along the west coast, creative engagement had been in full swing for centuries. As Vancouver looked through his wooden and brass telescope, he might have glimpsed pockets of anthropogenic grasslands—maintained by Coast Salish clans for food gathering and game draws—that grew along what is now Belltown.

The Coast Salish culture contained, and still contains, an aspect called kinscape[7]: family clans, intermarriage, extended families, and relationships spread out over large distances. Kinscape implies landscape as part of the fabric of relationship, an apt word for people for whom trees are kin, especially the western red cedars, *Thuja Plicata*—of the cypress family. *Xpay'uhc* as they call it, provided everything the local Snoqualmie indigenous people needed, from cradles to canoes to coffins, and are called trees of life. With their feathered and braided flat needles hung with tiny bell-like cones, and silvery trunks composed of fine linear rows of bark, the cedars stand like elegant dowagers throughout the forest. They expand to twenty-six feet in diameter and can survive up to 1500 years. Their fibrous longitudinal bark, stripped from the tree using a method that produced a long triangle but didn't harm the tree, was woven into mats, baskets, and bowls. They split whole planks for houses off trees using wedges in a manner that kept the tree alive. When needed, the taking of a whole tree with an intentional "cut" using fire took many days, but the whole being was used: thin roots outside the canopy circle woven into baskets, layered bark pounded into flexible clothing, trunks carved into shelter, or transport. The tree supported them, and they in turn honored the tree with respect and prayers.

One hundred years after Vancouver, creative engagement began to come to an end. US President John Quincy Adams wanted the expanding republic "to make the wilderness blossom as the rose...to subdue the earth." I pull out *A History of the Snoqualmie Valley* from my backpack. While settlers put their farms on native prairies in order to avoid intensive clearing of trees, (and plowed up camas and potatoes cultivated by natives in the process), others turned to the lumber trade. Male pioneers, gripped with orgiastic visions of wealth, cut, sawed, and axed their way into a frenzy that left behind a bare, smoking, dirt-floored landscape, ugly and barren to the point of despair. The photos reveal flatbed rail cars loaded with logs as big in diameter as small ponds, stacked and waiting to depart the forest. One cedar tree—over twenty-eight feet in circumference—shown flanked by two men, reduces them to ants next to a coffee can. North Bend had its famous Maloney's Grove along the South Fork of the Snoqualmie River, with rented cabins and amusements, and having your photo taken on Maloney's fir stump, nine feet across and over six hundred years old, seemed a right-of-passage for those who visited.

Because loggers started their cuts above where the trunk flared into the ground, they left stumps capacious enough to be made into homes, barns, and even a post office. The most colossal tree in the book grew in the Milwaukee Railroad right of way in the upper valley—somewhere between Snoqualmie and North Bend. Fifty feet around at ground level, a group of men worked shifts, over 24 hours, to fell the magnificent ĉǝbidac (pronounced che-*bee*-dotz), or Douglas fir. Eighty-four persons crowded onto the stump to pose for a photograph, with room for twenty more. The tree had been over a thousand years old; in its late middle-age, it could have thrived another five hundred years.

As commercial engagement replaced creative engagement, the trees seemed a never-ending supply of building materials to sell to a growing San Francisco to the south or shipped to places far flung as Hawaii. In the town where I live, originally called Tultxʷ but now known as Carnation, they scraped all the trees off the valley floor, then set up intensive farming practices for hops and cattle; timber camps sprouted at Lake Langlois, down at Griffin Creek, up Tolt Hill, and at Stillwater Hill in order to cut down the surrounding forest and create bare-naked hillsides. I imagine the trees as they succumbed to the ringing "misery whip" saws of the lumberjacks, as the great logs, defrocked of their massive branches (limbs that were themselves the diameter of trees), were skidded to the banks of the Tolt and Snoqualmie, floated downstream from forested slopes into the waiting arms of the sawmills. The source of all life here, our two rivers ended up carrying out their own dead, and then dying themselves, their waters silted by runoff and warmed by too much summer sun.

In Seattle, Yesler's Mill ran so long the tidal inlets on the Duwamish filled with sawdust, becoming known as Down on the Sawdust.[8] On most of the rivers that ran into Puget Sound, logging companies exploded rocks, broke up natural logjams from floods, and dammed up side channels which salmon used. They wanted fast water for floating timber. Here in the Snoqualmie Valley, twenty miles east of Yesler's mill, the denuded hillsides and bare riverbanks made the river a silted mess; with no logs to jam and slow the water for salmon fry, this meant faster, siltier water. Around the mill sites, the mountains of sawdust dumped into the water smothered salmon eggs and clogged the gills of dying fish.

The Snoqualmie, or sdukʷ albixʷ (pronounced roughly stuh-kwa-bew), and other indigenous peoples suffered many losses; perhaps the biggest one is loss of place, or loss of their "autochthonous rights" or the right to claim authentically to belong to this given area of forests, rivers, and abode of their ancestral spirits. By the early 1900's much of their land, stolen under the guise of federal treaties, lay in thrall to capitalism, and their beloved trees killed. I think of the modern day term solastalgia, which means a 'form of psychic or existential distress caused by environmental change.'[9] "The white men cut down all the great trees/And ran a railroad right through the land./Everyone was poor. Everyone helped everyone./I was midwife for my friend. And she was/midwife for me. We didn't give money to each other."[10] It's hard to imagine the distress they felt then, and feel today, caused by living in a kinscape-turned upside down, literally uprooted, from the ways they knew and still know.

What do these trees, the ones that remain, remember? Generations of indigenous placed their hands on their bark, hunted, prayed, buried their dead all around their feet or in their branches. Among their boughs, Douglas's squirrels or chicarees chattered and raised families; pileated woodpeckers and spotted owls nested in their cavities, and yellow-billed cuckoos and wood pigeons flocked throughout their canopies. I imagine the thousand-year-old tree in the photo, in this instance reduced to a flat gravestone of a stump, only multiplied. Over five thousand trees, some up to one thousand years old, all gone, reduced to discs spotting the ground like dinosaur footprints from here to the lip of the falls, and beneath the falls, throughout the lower valley where I live.

Today, the forests remain haunted by the ghosts of these giants. Many stumps, some still alive, are within walking distance of my home in the lower valley. The forest where I sit now, with the Mother tree nestled at my back, is dotted with them. Past and future intermingle, for often the deciduous ones like bigleaf maple have sprouted anew with fresh trunks that reach to the sky. If I'm haunted by the ghosts of the trees that once were, I'm drawn to those that escaped the misery whips, the steam donkey, and *Homo Sapiens Consumerii*. These aged trees are not paltry things. I'm entranced by these embattled, scarred survivors, maybe because I share their crenellated skin and rough, uncorked character of advanced age.

As I pack away my book and pull the rope from the Mother Tree, I think about how hard it is to imagine the diversity and density of the biomass contained in those ancient successional forests. One can get a narrow glimpse of how some forests may have looked in the deeper recesses of the middle fork of this same river: an understory thick with blowdowns, rotting logs, shelves of fungi ascending trunks, rills of tumbling water that feed into the river forks, an area rife with imagination, Bigfoot sightings, intense rainstorms, wildcats, bats, and owls. Mist and fog. But even there, it's mostly second growth.

What I longed to see was a forest of spirit. A forest—not just a single tree—that was like the old growth forests of old, where the trees grew large and fat like a stage set. As I stare off at a big stump with the characteristic springboard slots left by loggers, I think of the common forests in Europe, and of a book written by a German forest scientist, which argues, controversially--but only to a western mind--that plants are sentient, an idea shared by many cultures, and those of us who spend a lot of time in the outdoors. Ah, if only I knew a German forest scientist, I sniff.

I stand near Psilocybin Hill, looking southwest towards Paranoia Peak, somewhere near the Cascade crest and south of Interstate 90, close to the burble of Troublesome Creek. Fanged carnivores roam around these hills. It took an hour and a half drive in a utility truck on sewing-machine roads to get here, and rather than work the kinks out of our backs, we get out of the truck, walk through bear grass, burnt-orange tiger lilies, huckleberries, and piles of elk scat until we reach a tarn, or small mountain lake. Meadow grass surrounds the miniscule lake, and just beyond, mountain peaks rise straight up, covered with shaggy green spears of noble fir, Pacific Silver fir, mountain hemlock. To our left is a decayed log scratched open by an ant-seeking bear. We stand in a bowl of wilderness, two hors d'oeuvres on legs.

A tangible quiet pervades, punctured only by wing flaps, the buzzes of bees, dragonfly flybys, the audible swoops of swifts, and the whine of mosquitoes. Curtains of light hang over the bowl. A butterfly jitterbugs over the meadow; it's so quiet I hear it swallow. Annoyed squeaks rain down on us from a scree field above us, where picas, little rabbit cousins, make off-key notes as if blowing through duct-taped harmonicas. No human sounds exist here, save for our own thoughts.

That's because there are no cars allowed in this, the Cedar River Watershed, save for the vehicles of a handful of workers, spread over 600 miles of networked roads. No people allowed in here period--present company excluded. That means no hiking trails, nor any of the million hikers who inhabit Seattle, no pocketbook carrying, gum-chewing general public, no tourists Instagramming themselves while ignoring don't-pick-the-wildflower signs, no *Homo sapiens consumerii,* no rugged individualist overnight campers. And while we are at it, no serial killers, no oil lobbyists, no drunken inner-tube floaters. Miracle of miracles, even the logging companies have been thrown out. And because this unpeopled wilderness of 90,546 acres of forest, lakes, and rivers is a protected, gravity-fed, naturally filtered water supply for 1.5 million parched Seattleites, no human bodily functions allowed, either. Instead, there's thirty or more port-o-potties spread over miles that must be used no exceptions, should I--a writer with a hyped up endocrine system and a sprained foot--need to eliminate the gallon of coffee I drank on the way in to fix my caffeine-to-hemoglobin ratio. Fortunately for me, we passed one such *el banyo plastico* on the way up. It was so clean you could throw a dinner party inside.

What *is* here is old growth, high on the mountain tops. 14,000 delicious acres of it which my host has invited me to sample, but not before we gaze upon this diamond of a tarn. I'm mere miles from the upper plateau of my valley, less than thirty miles, as the heron flies, from my home. As we stare at the water the stillness feels as deep as the reflection of the mountains. Time measures itself in wing-beats here. It's so quiet, I find myself wondering if we are the last two people in the world and after I left home this morning all nuclear hell broke loose. Then my host's radio squawks, and I jump ten feet in the air.

This lovely, non-peopled wilderness, owned by the City of Seattle, has roughly forty-five employees. Many of them work on a road crew that, short of vacuuming and dusting the roads, makes sure there is no runoff, road sediment, or general crud which might contaminate the water supply. They track, measure, repair, buttress, study, and all but lick clean the byways in here, which are with minor exceptions, unpaved and thus permeable to water. Then there are the four to five staff who study and track the nature of this place, who try to understand what is going on with forest succession and lake ecology, and how it is changing. One of whom is my host, Rolf Gersonde, who happens to have been born and raised in West Berlin. A German forest scientist. An ecologist, to be precise.

I am here to help him take line transects of an old growth plot at 3,500 feet and hope I don't become a government experiment on how best to impale oneself on Devil's Club. Earlier, when I met him at the entrance gates, the Grimm's Fairy Tales part of my brain expected a roly-poly 80-year-old man with an axe over his shoulder. Mildly surprised by a 58-year-old athletic scientist with a waterproof iPad and the physique of someone who could climb the Matterhorn in fourteen minutes, the other thing I didn't expect this morning was a cliff.

The county I live in stretches from the coast to the Cascades, and resembles a trapezoid drawn by a drunken sawyer. Home to creatures as varied as seals, salmon, mountain goats, whales, and some rapidly melting glaciers, it's also home to 2,269,675 soggy, overcaffeinated humans, and six watersheds fed by the giant water collectors, the Central Cascades. The Cedar River Watershed's protected area is twice the size of a small European country. The protected part starts in meadows near the crest of the mountains, and becomes less protected, and more populated, as it spans the county west to the Salish Sea. Shaped like a banana, it includes 14 creeks, 3 lakes, and an inhabited island for the well-to-do. It includes Lake Washington which buffers us 'east-siders' from Seattle, a lake that represents a geographic social divide that Seattle-ites prefer never to cross.

My watershed—the Snoqualmie—intersects with this one, the Cedar River, in North Bend, just along Rattlesnake Lake. That was where Rolf picked me up earlier today at a set of double gates at 7:30 am, but not before I had technically committed a misdemeanor and eliminated some coffee behind some shrubs.

We cleared several electronic entrance gates and began our climb into the Cascades. As we zigzagged up forest service roads--left, right, switchback, ascent--the road diverged often enough I lost my sense of direction. Rolf didn't consult any maps-- this place was mapped on his heart, a small world he knew really well, but a world, too, he told me this morning in his low, gentle cadence, of responsibility, of good stewardship of the land.

"We have a mandate from the people. I'm not doing this for myself."

A stunning, long blue lake appeared, embedded in the forest below. We drove alongside it for what seemed like a long time. The lake's real name, Nooknu, means *place where the water gathers*. In 1889 after Seattle suffered a devastating fire, some enterprising folks wanted to create a water supply for the city. They focused on this natural groundwater lake, and installed a masonry dam, which drowned some forest and several small towns, before it created the much larger Chester Morse Lake, which took the shape of a long, blue multi-pronged ghost. The water, by the time it left here, was screened, chlorinated, fluoridated, ozonated, disinfected, and supplemented with lime to prevent lead-pipe leaching. But inside the watershed protection zone it was still wild, tinged with moss and stone. Ralph stopped the truck at a roadside cascade pouring over some mossed rocks. He has imbibed the water from this natural spring for ten years.

"Of course, you take your own risk," he quipped with a grin as he jumped into the gully and held the container under the rill.

As we ascended the twisted ridges, the lanes grew more primitive, and the forest grew younger. Before logging was discontinued, each drainage had been logged west to east, except for the tops of the mountains and high ridges, which the logging companies couldn't reach. That's where most of the old growth lived now. He stopped the truck and pointed to a ridge across the lake. About 1/3 of the way down the ridge, he indicated with a wave of his hand where a dark band of trees, a ragged layer of Noble and Pacific fir lived. The trees had broken, rebuilt crowns, and bore signs of a lifetime of insect infestation, heavy snow loads, winds, and disease. Their greenery looked patched and clumped. Old growth.

The raggedness of these trees, he explained, was part of the interplay of an old growth forest, "the building and restoring that the forests do as a whole." He pointed to another layer just below the old growth, where the trees rose in perfect, symmetrical spears: second growth. Then he put the truck in gear.

As the truck climbed the road, I ask him how he ended up here, in this little corner of the US. When Rolf was young, he often spent time in West Berlin's parks by himself, but his family also valued outdoorsmanship; later, after college, he ended up working for the forest industry in Washington, amidst concerns about forest declines in Europe, and acid rain on the East Coast. In 1998 he earned a degree from UC Berkeley, in Environmental Science Policy and Management, then got hired by the watershed. He and his wife have lived in North Bend, in the upper Snoqualmie Valley, ever since. His wife ran a well-stocked, popular general store near Rattlesnake Lake, where Rolf also sold used mountaineering books and literature on the outdoors. I knew it well.

We continued to bump and rise in elevation. Rolf took left and right forks without slowing, while I followed on my map. The watershed was a place of beauty and almost military-style surveillance: down by Rattlesnake Lake, a computer tracked our location. In case of a rollover, or accident, they could find us, or if we went AWOL, which is what I'd like to do.

This part of the watershed, like all the watersheds in the county, had been in continuous use by various indigenous groups for hunting, gathering, and vision quests. As we neared the Cascade crest and made a hairpin turn, I asked where the original footpath over the mountains was (it's not where I-90 cuts through the pass). Rolf pointed down below us to an inviting meadow dotted with evergreens, where he believed the ancient pathway, still visible in some places, existed. Soon the road turned up and south. On our right the forest grew dense and dark. The boles, tightly packed together, resembled a forest drawn in charcoal pencil, no sunlight, no understory; just a dark, uninviting woodland. This was what second growth looked like up close; most hikers encountered similar patches within the Cascades. It looked barren. "The loggers removed all the slash and deadfall; with no slash, there's no understory. When they burned the slash it became a homogenous seedbed, a monoculture of about 1,000 trees per acre."

He gestured out his window to the opposite side of the road, which they had thinned to mimic a more natural environment, as if it hadn't ever been logged: huckleberry, Devils club, red flowering currant, ferns, vanilla leaf, and mosses made a green undulating carpet in between trees. The deciduous foliage dropped off each fall, provided micro-nutrients to the soil, and built up organic matter. The plants provided 15-25% of the nutrients the trees needed, and helped the forest grow up. It also made better habitat for insects, for birds to fly through and forage in, and for browse for deer and elk and myriad mammal species. "We thinned this area down to about 400 trees per acre, but in some cases that's not good enough." To look back and forth from the lush side to the dark, barren upright trunks on the other, was a contrast in ideologies.

As if to prove his point we startled a Barred Owl perched near the road. The owl made several short, twisted flights around the dark boles to our right in the barren ugly forest, then spied on us from a branch. "It's not easy for the owl to navigate through that thicket of trunks, but he'll still hunt in there if he has to."

Which brings me to the heavily forested cliff Rolf has just parked alongside of. After we left the peacefully quiet tarn, we drove a quarter mile back down the road. At the bottom of the cliff, in a steep forested bowl, lies one of a hundred plus forest plots he studies. Every ten years he and a small crew measure various things within each plot; it takes them three years to collect information from all the plots. Before we hop out and don our backpacks he turns and says with a glint in his eye:

"It's time to turn the forest into numbers."

In the truck bed: an odd assortment of PVC pipes, wires, a utility bucket, pieces of metal. It looks like we are about to build a satellite. He starts pulling pipes out—some have black, red, and white increments marked on them, others are blank. He hands me two six-foot sections—"You can use these as hiking sticks," he says half joking in accented English, then picks up the rest and points to where we are going: through a line of thick trees and boulders, straight down into the ravine. Or cliff. There's no clear way to get through the line of trees, and no way to know if the route you've chosen will result in a good descent. His pale blue eyes narrow as he smiles.

"At some point, you just need to commit," he laughs as we walk along the edge of the road, and with that, he disappears through the scrub. Between the terrain and the predators, I'm glad he showed me where the keys to the truck are kept. Rolf is almost a third of the way down the slope before I fight my way through the line of trees and boulders—I'm only five foot one--and start to descend into the north-facing ravine. I follow him down, sprained foot and all, as he hops over blow downs, balances on downed trees, crunches through huckleberry and ferns up to our necks, until we stop near the bottom of a green bowl of forest.

He's looking for markers—flagging, PVC pipes sticking out of the ground, or worse, bare rebar, which delineates the transect line. Bare rebar? I'm informed it's poking up out of the ground all over—invisible of course in forest duff—but most notably on the downed tree bole I'm balancing on. Lucky for me, some rebar is covered by white PVC pipes, and pink flagging marks others. Rolf thrashes around to find the center of the 70-meter measurement area. He crunches back and we dump the gear and pipes in a small clearing.

Rolf dons a vest with pockets, loops a stylus around his neck, and tucks a hammer into a pocket sewn into the vest's back. Until he gets his transect lines set up and his first set of measurements entered into his iPad, he tells me I'm free to "get to know the forest." While he approximates the canopy cover with a small, curved mirror marked with grid lines, fitted into his palm, I stand in a patch of sun under a canopy opening.

In this north-facing ravine, shocks of light pour onto the forest floor, and Greeklike columns of silver trunks thrust skyward to stupefying heights. The canopy holds its palms up towards invisible stars. Looking north through the forest I see bright sun-plashed meadows. The air looks and smells green. Here, time acts more like brightness or loudness, more magnitude than currency.

Far below the treetops, I swim in a leafy sea. Huckleberry bushes grow over my head, and I could drown in the clumps of sword fern, some of which grow to Carboniferous proportions. I thrash around for a while, then work my way over to a clearing, past knee-high shrubs of silver fir. At my feet, False hellebore, with its large curvilinear emerald leaves and poisonous black rhizomes, sprouts from a moist seep on the forest floor, and a host of vanilla leaf with their tri-leaf patterns forms a herd of little moose heads around my ankles. Myriad ferns stick up like green feather dusters, and though it's early August, at this elevation the lime green of new growth or spring fir tips--which make a bracing tea--remain visible on little fir seedlings. The pendulous cones of Pacific Silver Fir *(Abies amabilis)* Grand Fir *(Abies grandis)* and Douglas Fir *(Pseudotsuga menziesii)* litter the ground in armloads. Half-discs of artist fungus or bear bread stick out from dead trees. I thrash back into the understory, then submerge: down on my hands and knees I smell dark mold, imagine roots gently probing the soil.

Bees and wasps and horseflies zip around, their wings ablur. From the forest edge comes the "quick THREE beers" of an Olive sided flycatcher, hawking for insects. Then the descending vee-eer call of nighthawks, a bird shaped like a little boomerang usually heard at dusk. In the ancient quiet, I hear sunlight filtering through the canopy, the whine of mosquitoes, fungus growing, elk scat decaying. I hear the plink of fir needles as they fall every few moments like rain. Intermittently, I hear Rolf crunching around like the bear that I joked earlier will come and eat him, and leave me stranded, hopefully for the rest of my life.

I resurface, walk over to where we left our gear, and slowly swivel my head around like an owl to look at this patch of old growth woodland. I don't want to tell Rolf, but I'm disappointed. These aren't the fat boles of old growth I was expecting. I've been spoiled by my verdigris fantasies of what used to thrive on the valley floor, the tantalizing photographs of ancient diverse stands made obese by a diet of water by the ton, and alluvial minerals by the mountain-load. I wanted woods like Vancouver and Wilkes saw, what the Coast Salish people knew, woods that held multilayered canopies like green clouds and trunks big around as a circus tent. Here the old growth looks....dare I say, skinny. The trees, around 350 years old, started out life during the Little Ice Age. At this altitude, above 3,000 feet, they live on an anorexic diet of long winters, cool summers, and lack the alluvial soil and volumes of water that their cousins in the lowlands have in abundance. Their trunks look thin. Though they lack the buttressed bases and width of age you'd see on the valley floor, some of the trees can grow to a thousand years old or more. Each tree wears a silver numbered tag: with their dangling earrings, they are the arboreal equivalent of aging supermodels.

Rolf finishes his first set of survey data. We have a snack (carrots for him, chocolate for me, revealing deeply held priorities). Then he takes four pipes and fits them into a 4' x 4' square, and I discover what all this rebar is for: he attaches one corner of the square to the rebar that sticks up along the transect line. Within each quadrant, we measure and estimate percentages of moss, herbs, and shrubs. Rolf calls out the four-letter species codes, and as I enter them into the iPad, the plants begin to separate into distinct individuals, each square of leafy vegetation revealing a world of delicate beings.

The maroon spires of the saprophytic Western coralroot, which lacks the ability to make its own food and depends on decaying organic matter to survive; two different kinds of huckleberry, distinguishable by subtle variations in leaf shape and taste; Queens cup lilies, with their ovate leaves sticking out of the ground in a whorl, their single white starshaped flowers already come and gone, and the clustered leaves of Dwarf bramble, whose berries are said to "miniaturize the essence of raspberry flavour (sic) as perfectly as wild strawberries do the essence of strawberry."[11] There's Rosy Twisted-stalk, with its long arching unbranched stem, though I have to imagine its little rose and white flower bells, and Five-leaved bramble or creeping raspberry, whose five leaves resemble a toe-print.

Nothing goes unremarked: leaf litter, rocks, moss, plants, even decaying tree trunks noted and measured for their rate of decline. I feel a marked sense of renewal helping to attend to the details of identification, the sparse fringes of hair at the nodes, whether a stalk is slender or fat, or a leaf shiny or matte, and whether the flowers have produced berries yet. If some plants were strangers to me, even as I reduce them to percentages in a square, a kinship develops just in the act of looking, of noticing, as if I were now at a reunion of friends. All the foliage is flecked and glistening with sugar from the aphids high above us sucking on the tree canopy.

Rolf has looked at historic photographs of various parts of this watershed in detail. His observations reveal that what stays relatively static at a larger scale—old trees, young trees, understory species—remains, at a smaller scale, very dynamic. Trees live in a different time scale than their frenetic, watch-obsessed human counterparts: two thirty has as much meaning here as a pair of cufflinks. If you could look at a forest through time lapse photography, and condense one hundred years down to a minute, you'd see vegetation and trees growing and decaying in rapid jerk-filled movements. But viewed through a human lens, trees appear sloth-like.
In this sea-light, surrounded by this grove of jewelry-obsessed supermodels who move in their own time zone, a strange flicker of thought washes over me. If relation is mutual, if, as Ellen Meloy writes, kindship demands reciprocity, it occurs to me that maybe the plot is measuring us, not vice versa. What kind of awareness, I wonder, do the plants carry of us, as we move along with our quadrant, careful not to step on any?

Over lunch (fancy cheese sandwich with greens for him, squashed peanut butter for me), Rolf tells me how the field of ecology—objective science--defines an old growth forest. It has to have been primary forest, having never been harvested and therefore relatively free of human interference. It has to be in 'late seral stage' where trees like Doug fir are gradually replaced by silver fir and hemlock. And my personal favorite, it has to have decadence. By decadence, Rolf refers to the standing dead trees that have come to the end of their natural lifespan, and the decaying logs necessary for regeneration of new life. I love the word: my mind flashes on trees shooting heroin, robbing convenience stores, and driving into the city in logging trucks so they can fall on people. Rolf's point: while some second growth trees are bigger in diameter than some of the old growth here, this plot contains something second growth stands lack; a complexity and thus a stability that begins to come into partial view when you turn the forest into numbers.

As I sit in the coolness, I feel the interconnectedness and the quiet wonders of this place. Beyond the plant communities, the architecture of old growth—shaggy, clumped crowns, tops that become more rounded, deadfalls that create openings, help a host of wildlife to thrive: bats can glide through openings in branches and canopy, owls can hunt more freely. Truffles thrive in the old mycorrhiza, which are eaten by flying squirrels, who are in turn eaten by spotted owls. Insects love the crevices and messiness in which they hide, breed, and hunt. The canopy shelters Swainsons thrushes, while the lower reaches of trunks, with cavities and crevasses, create homes for red squirrels, or chicarees. Little teacup wrens live in the foliage lower down. The web of connection unfolds a map wide in all directions: the marbled murrelet flies twenty miles inland from the Salish Sea to lay a single egg in a depression on the wide, lichened branches of old growth; it will fly out to the sea to feed, and comes back at night to incubate its brown-flecked orb. Science only 'discovered' the marbled murrelet's nesting habits recently. What else don't we understand?

The tangled thickets of sword fern are food for the mountain beavers, living fossils who dig holes in the soft soil with their Yoda-like fingers and live under tree roots near seeps and streams. Banana slugs cruise the dense floor, turning dead leaves and animal feces into a glistening rich soil. And, of course, as we breathe out, the trees breathe in, and turn carbon dioxide into oxygen.

As we eat and talk, surrounded by hordes of vanilla leaf, used indoors for its vanilla scent, and Indian hellebore, or Corn Lilly, a "violently poisonous" plant, used for a variety of medicinal uses, I think of this plot, what Rolf calls a reference condition or reference plot. Rolf tries to make sense of what's happening here. Most of the forest in the watershed is mid-seral or 70-80 years old, and as he explains, they want it to move into the late seral stage. In other words, how does a second growth forest, decimated by logging and devoid of what a forest needs, like the dark forest by the roadside we passed earlier, develop complexity and stability like the one we're sitting in? Surrounded by traditional medicinal plants, and trees that provide shelter, it's hard not to think of the older lifeways as those that guide us towards those two things—complexity, stability-- lifeways that were scraped away just like forest duff during the European land scramble of the past 170 years.

We finish our sandwiches and take up the quadrant again, moving east along the transect line. In the vespertine light, the sounds of birdsong and insect wings, no longer plangent, become woolly, as if we're underwater. I feel myself edging into bottle-green torpor as we wade through shrubs that resemble green spindrift. I've breathed in so many phytochemicals I feel high.

The hours tick by, and the sun trickles through different parts of the canopy in the late afternoon. The supermodels with their frothy skirts of understory have a narcotic effect; time loosens from its strictures. We take a walk around, for the old growth extends far beyond the plot lines. We tiptoe among the plants towards a ravine, where a stream meanders, fed by the little tarn we visited. Taking careful steps, Rolf explains he likes to see what else is here, outside the boundaries of the transect lines, and I can tell he enjoys the respite from percentages, from objectivity. Surprises abound. He points out this or that plant, then he tells me there could be orchids. These are not the showy hothouse supermarket floozies in Trader Joe's. They are subtle, tiny.

What's this, I ask, pointing to a thin green fuzzy stick less than a foot high, with pale green yellow flowers dotting its top half. They look less like flowers than little traps. Up close, very close, there are horn-like teeth at the base of each trap. "Well, hello there," he says to the plant. An orchid. The orchid is likely a Northwestern Twayblade, or *Listera caurina*. It's a stick with attitude: some twayblades blow their pollen out explosively so as to glue it to unsuspecting insects. It occurred to me that this is the poetry of survival, a forest of spirit. And also, the precious little things—stems that sneeze pollen—that the logging companies decimate when they "harvest" a forest, and that developers in the lowlands kill when they raze land to erect giant box-like homes.

Too soon, we have to go, so we gather the pipes and gear and hike back up the cliff. Surprisingly we emerge close to the truck. I ask if he can take me back to the little tarn before we leave, knowing I may never see this place again. He agrees, of course, and we drive back up. The bowl lies bathed in golden light, the tarn at its center like earth's green eye. As we wander, we find mosquito larval casings left as high-water marks on a rock by the lake, and walk through violets. The band of pikas shriek at us again. The sun lights up a meadow behind the trees, halfway up the mountain beyond; it casts the opening in a buttery light: a hidden meadow, invisible in this morning's sun, now visible, but out of reach like a dream.

As Rolf guides the truck downhill on the graveled byways, he tells me that many years ago he began conversations with some economists about the ecological system services that the Cedar River Watershed provides. The economists did some analysis and discovered that the intrinsic benefits to humans, or the non-monetary values, outstripped the value of the forest as extractive goods. As he explains it, the 'existence value' of this place also has emotional value, and the economists were able to put a price tag on it.

I nod in agreement as the blur of green rolls by the windows. It reminds me of the way the Coast Salish think when they speak about the emotional pricelessness of their ancestral lands. We come around a bend and a fat marmot sits by the side of the road, then flies up in the air. We've discovered a new species: a winged forest-marmot. But no. It's another barred owl. Around another turn, we startle three ruffed grouse, who scramble up into the undergrowth.

He unhooks the radio and lets the central office know we'll be out soon—everyone has to be out of the watershed by 6 pm. He squints as we head into a sunlit portion of road, one hand on the wheel.
"Nowadays expectations are different. We call that the "shift in baseline." When my daughter, who is 17, was born, we used to see people lined up all along the Lake Washington bridge into Seattle, fishing for sockeye. Since 2006 we haven't seen that.

My daughter won't know what it's like. Today, tree mortality is common. People get used to things being the way they are, because they don't remember any other way." In other words, since all of our thousand-year-old trees, the ones that diminished us to the size of ants, have mostly been cut down (and to see one today takes effort), people don't miss their presence.

What am I in search of when I seek old trees? When I look at old photos of gigantic boles, so fat they reduce humans to miniscule specks, I'm seized with a nostalgia I cannot name. Perhaps because these trees, with their Hollywood-on-steroids, Jack-and-the-Beanstalk size, dwarf any human endeavor. When we lived in and among large plants, life had the grace that humility brought, and the giants reminded us of wonder.
Lately, the cadre of man-children who rule Silicon Valley have determined that the human race should ride in self-driving cars, live in a metaverse rather than reality, and worse, go live on Mars. One toxic capitalist wizard has declared that life on other planets will be necessary in order to preserve human "consciousness." Man has become so afraid of nature he requires whole planets between him and greenery. Never mind that gravity is essential to having skeletal systems that function, and that greenery and nature is part of the poetry of our survival, Silicon Valley envisions us better off as withered, gelid hominids staring into screens while sitting in a barren landscape at -80 Fahrenheit. These scenarios also neglect that with our precious "consciousness," we will be the first species to witness our own extinction.

I'd rather clothe myself in cedar bark and goat hair, eat dried huckleberry cakes, make vessels out of fine roots and grasses than to go live on Mars. When I can't face humanity's inane antics anymore, I slither out the door before my own skeleton turns into jelly and my brain descends into blubber-brained insanity, and return to the old technologies: my legs, a pen, a notebook. I return to the Mother Tree at the Twin Falls trail.

Rolf knows this tree as well, he thinks it's a fine old tree, and he agreed with my age assessment of at least five hundred years, which pleased me. Of Susan Simard's work, he believes it is groundbreaking. I lean my back against the Mother tree's flaky skin and place my derriere back over the mining operation. Simard aptly points out that above and below ground, a forest has the same pattern as a neural network; some of the compounds that trees exchange, are the same as some neurotransmitters in the human brain.

While trees may not have a brain, she says, "Plants perceive, receive information, and make decisions. They have memories. They can learn. These are all attributes we ascribe to intelligence...all those abilities and skills evolved over hundreds of millions of years." And while humans "came along much later in evolutionary history...the origin of [tree and plant] intelligence is much more complex and not that much different than we find in human beings."[12]

Science cautions us against anthropomorphizing. It's even, according to many in the white male echelon that has dominated the genre, the big 'no-no' of nature writing. But for a species built on stories, we require metaphors. I can't help but think that metaphors bring us into equality with the world. They allow us to imagine beyond our rigid scientific definitions, to other possibilities, to acknowledge that, yes, trees have intelligence. This is how the First Nations people view trees, and how Greek philosophers did, like Pliny the Elder, who attributed sense, and spirit, to plants.

All I know this morning, as I sit with my back up against the tree with my eyes closed is this: while I can help turn a forest into numbers to better understand its lifeways, the language of numbers only takes humans so far. My childhood, steeped as it was in the language of science, lacked words to describe the mysteries and awe I felt in a forest. While the *Life Nature Library* series my father owned had opened the door to nature for me as a child, science, with its insistence on dry theoretical frameworks, fell woefully short for me on imagination. Imagination marches right up to the borders of science, and occasionally, bursts through, as when Simard wondered if trees nurtured instead of competed.

Many indigenous cultures combine imagination with deep knowledge, reflected in their language, such as the Potawatomi word *puhpowee*, which describes "the force which causes mushrooms to push up from the earth overnight."[13] Potawatomi Nation member Robin Wall Kimmerer's question in *Braiding Sweetgrass*, what if nature loves us back? is the reciprocal part of the poetry of survival. We've forgotten we are a part of something that provides for us: bacteria that keep us alive live in our gut and on our skin; trees that provide oxygen, wood for houses, and food to eat. The loss we incur after the land of the giants has been all cut down is the loss of what makes us human: the love we would have gotten if we treated nature right, if we allowed nature to love us back. To turn a tree into a 'thing,' or a forest into numbers, is to obfuscate what it is: kith and kin.

In my numerous visits to the Mother Tree, I've never seen her crown. My observations stopped at the point where her main leader had cracked off, leaving the jagged impression she was in decline. I assumed the green boughs I saw near her top were from the trees around her, or were other species living off her decay. I decide to take a better look. I amble through the understory fifty feet in various directions, and glass her crown from different vantage points, against a backdrop of birdsong and the susurrus of the South Fork.

A fat bole rises another thirty feet into the sky beyond the cracked off part. A number of branches and greenery adorn her top. I zoom in on one of the green boughs and bring the foliage into focus. The whorls of needles go all the way around the stem. Not flat, like hemlock. Definitely Doug fir.

The Mother Tree is alive.

Endnotes

1 It's a case study in why we need more women (as well as people of color) in science: people with different cultural experiences, such as Native Americans, have life experiences that exist well outside the dominant societal, religious, cultural, political, and scientific, "norm," so they naturally, with their different life experiences, ask different questions than the standard, lab-coated white guys.

2 Seattle Times Staff, "Giant Logged Long Ago, Not Forgotten," *The Seattle Times*, September 4, 2011, updated September 5, 2011, https://www.seattletimes.com/life/giant-logged-long-ago-but-not-forgotten/.

3 "II. Seeing the forest for the Trees: Placing Washington's Forests in Historical Context," Center for the Study of the Pacific Northwest, University of Washington, Accessed April 4, 2022, https://www.washington.edu/uwired/outreach/cspn/Website/Classroom%20Materials/Curriculum%20Packets/Evergreen%20State/Section%20II.html.

4 Tom Schroeder, Pre-Settlement Forests Around Puget Sound: Eyewitness Evidence, April 22, 2022, https://www.biorxiv.org/content/10.1101/592733v5.

5 "Seeing the Forest for the Trees."

6 "Pre-settlement Forests Around Puget Sound."

7 Word from *Over the Falls* by Jay Miller, usage mine.

8 Murray Morgan, "One Man's Seattle" in *Skid Road*, Revised edition, (New York: Viking Press, 1960), Page 9.

9 Robert McFarland, "The Edge" in *Underland*, (New York: W.W.Norton & Company, Ltd, First American Edition, 2019) p. 317.

10 Patrick Twohy, "At Home No Longer" in *Beginnings, A Meditation on Coast Salish Lifeways*, (LaConnor, WA: Patrick Twohy, Second Edition 2003), p. 64. The quote is from Marya Moses, Snohomish.

11 Jim Pojar, Andy MacKinnon, *Plants of the Pacific Northwest Coast: Washington, Oregon, British Columbia & Alaska,* compiled and edited by Pojar and MacKinnon (Canada: BC Ministry of Forests and Lone Pine Publishing, 1994) p. 79.

12 Susan Simard, *Treeline: The Secret Life of Trees,* (directed by Jordan Manley, produced by Laura Yale and Monika McClure), Patagonia Films, January 27, 2019, film on YouTube, accessed September 12, 2023, https://www.youtube.com/watch?v=YCEaYInJbos.

13 Robin Wall Kimmerer, "Learning the Grammar of Animacy" in *Braiding Sweetgrass*, (Minneapolis: Milkweed Editions, 2013), p. 49.

Beaver Moon
Finalist in the Derick Burleson Poetry Contest

Christine Andersen

Its round silence stuns me.

November's full moon
hovers over the woods
lighting the tips of the bare branches,
floats in the pool
the beavers made with their dam.

In summer we laughed
when a furry twosome
belly-flopped off the bank,
tails slapping the lazy surface
with a splash that rained down
a waterfall of crystals,
bubbles riding expanding circles.
Their merriment was a gift
we carried home.

One late October afternoon,
we watched as a tree was felled,
gnawed at the bottom
to fine points
like the crux of an hourglass—
the beavers with their mounded bodies,
buck teeth and broad tails,
waddling,
hauling and gathering,
layering branches,
preparing for the deep freeze.

When I crawled into bed,
I thought of them laboring
through the night.
I felt a kinship.
Don't we all work to survive?

Under this ripe November moon
the beavers swim into their lodges
built log upon log, stick upon stick.
Settle in.
Savor a hard-won feast.

Candy Clouds
Finalist in the Mary Cassatt Art Contest

Jordyn-Elizabeth Pimental

Christmas in Dubai, 2011
2ⁿᵈ place in the Phil Heldrich Nonfiction Contest

Sara R. Sands

* All names have been changed for privacy.

"The presents do not wrap themselves," Raga* says, handing me scissors, tape, and three rolls of Christmas-themed wrapping paper. "Thank you for your help." I look up at her from my newly-designated seat, sprawled out on the Persian silk carpet on the floor. She sits down on the sofa - a very old, expensive antique that cost her a fortune to reupholster in such a fine jacquard. It is beige with dark wood and matches the other beige and dark wood things all set against olive green walls. She leans over, resting her head for a moment on Kynan's shoulder. He is reading a thick book with the enticing title, *Tort Law: Cases, Perspectives, and Problems.*

"Look at my son," she turns to me. "You know how I know he is training to be a lawyer?"

"Because it is two days before Christmas and he is reading about torts instead of making tortes?" I ask.

"No," she says, very serious. "It is the first time that he has a belly," lightly tapping his stomach. "Look at the small belly starting," she says to Kynan. "Just like your father. Has he gotten fatter from all that drinking?"

"Thank you, Mum," he says, snapping shut the book and standing to leave. "Now if you don't mind, I think I'll continue revising in my room."

"Oh, my son, I am so proud of you. You go study, and we will wrap the presents and make a big display under the tree for you. Or perhaps you can come back in a bit and help us? Presents do not wrap themselves."

She sits down cross-legged on the floor with me, forming a human archipelago in a sea of shopping bags from stores with names I either can't pronounce or can't afford. Everybody already knows what they are getting. Earlier that day, Santa the Middleman was cut out. Instead, Raga, Kynan, and I piled into the Jaguar and cruised to the source–the Dubai Mall. Even Duaa, Raga's Filipino maid–a must have for every Dubai family, I'm told–had come with us and picked out her own gift, a new mobile phone with which to call home. Christmas morning would be a perfunctory exercise of unwrapping presents for the sake of snapping feigned surprise photos and reciting the inscriptions on cards.

Not that it matters much to me one way or the other. This is not my holiday, and technically, it isn't Raga's either. After the divorce, Kynan's dad, the Irish Catholic parent, went back to England. She stayed in Dubai to run her marriage counseling and psychology clinic and re-joined the Iranian mosque.

"Can you please pass me the scissors and the jingle bells paper?" she asks. "With the two of us, we'll be done in no time."

I brought the menorah because I couldn't not bring one. My family had shipped from the U.S. to the U.K. two menorahs. The first one we received was from my grandmother in Phoenix, who had sent us a glass Chanukah menorah ornament from a special Hallmark collection to hang on the tree. The package also included a Christmas tree-shaped guitar that played "Jingle Bell Rock." The two together were a sort of peacemaking exercise – a symbolic gesture to signify her acceptance that I may not marry a Jewish man.

My mother then sent a small travel menorah she purchased from our synagogue gift shop in New Orleans. It had a big Star of David in the middle and blue and white Chanukah candles that were really just birthday candles with different packaging. This is the one I packed.

"It is Chanukah over Christmas this year. Did you know that?"

"No, Mom," I didn't. It was 1 o'clock in the afternoon in London and all I knew was I was hungover and the plate of beans-on-toast in front me, a Kynan favorite, resembled vomit.

"Yes, and do you know how long it has been since a member of our family lit Chanukah candles in the Middle East? In an Arab country?"

"No, Mom. How long?"

"Since your great-grandparents left Syria and moved to America. That's how long. Do you have a menorah? Do you have Chanukah candles? I'll send them."

Kynan had rolled his eyes when he saw me putting them in the suitcase the night before the trip. At passport control, queued up behind an Indian family dressed in saris all the shades of a 64-pack of Crayola crayons, he just about lost his shit over it.

"Between that and your Israeli stamps, you're going to get sent back," he fretted.

"No, I won't," I said. "Money is the common language here, and I guarantee you that Dubai wants my money more than they hate the Jews."

It should not be important, but if we're keeping score, I was right.

"After we had the little-er one," Raga says, referring to her second child, Kynan's middle sister, Mary, "Paul would not let me buy pads for my menstruation. I cut out the bottom of diapers and taped them into my panties."

I'm gliding the scissors across the necks of Rudolph and the gang on the wrapping paper. She is picking up the conversation from the point where she stopped the other night while we were waiting for 30 minutes to try to park at the Gold Souk because I had to see it, we could not *just come back*, and besides, she wanted to ask about some Colombian emeralds.

From my computer speakers, Ella Fitzgerald croons "let it snow." The seagulls outside rise up from the sand in a cloud.

"He served me the papers on Valentine's Day. Did Kynan tell you that?" she asks, referring to the divorce papers from her ex-husband.

"Yes," I nod. "He did."

"It was my first day at chemotherapy. He was my cancer though. It was in my breast and in my home. I got rid of both. I survived both."

"Of course, the bigger one," referring to her first child, Kynan's oldest sister, Katherine, "went with him. As a child, she would take photos of me and poke pins through my eyes. She belongs to her father."

On the mantelpiece at Paul's house in England, there is a picture of his new girlfriend, Carrie. Only for well over a year I didn't know it was Carrie. It looked so much like Raga. I didn't register the difference until, jobless, homeless, and nearly penniless, Paul took us in for the summer. (F)un-employed, I had enough time to stare at the collection of pictures, tchotchkes, and books crammed onto the shelves. It turns out Carrie and Raga come from the same village in Northern Iran, located so close to Azerbaijan that as children they spoke Persian and Azerbaijani as their first and second languages.

"When Kynan came to visit me after I got out of the hospital from my first round of chemo, I came out of the clinic with my head scarf on because I had no hair. I thought I looked okay, but when he saw me there were tears in his eyes."

She is waiting for my response, but I don't have one. I don't have the right one, anyway. She takes that as a sign to continue.

"Every night we would sit on that sofa, and he would read me poems from my favorite Iranian poets and he would stroke my head scarf so I could go to sleep."

Five candles burn in the menorah I lit as the sun was going down. The light of the moon is deflected by the waves.

"I do this," she says, pointing to the tree adorned in red and gold and the gifts and the fine silver, already on the table waiting to be set, "for Kynan, my youngest child, my only good child. My good son."

I take a deep breath. She seems used to this discomfort, like someone who walks around in a hazmat suit all the time.

"I think your daughters miss you," I say. "They admire you greatly. They know you are so brave and so smart, and I think you might find that they are not the same people they were five years ago."

"It cannot be," she says. "That is just what you want to believe."

"I have saved a bottle of wine for the two of you for tomorrow night," Raga tells me. "It is from a patient. He gave it to me last year for Christmas, but I do not drink now that Kynan's father is gone," pausing like a widow remembering. "I hope it will be good. If it is not good, I will be angry. It is so risky for me to even have alcohol."

"I'm sure it will be wonderful," I say.

I wrap Kynan's Massimo Dutti boots, the brown leather belt, and the jacket that is part-gray wool blazer and part-black hoodie. One of those clothing items that looks like you put on two things when you only put on one, and seems like it could be warm, but actually falls short of its intended purpose. Even men sacrifice functionality for fashion.

Raga is writing a card.

"Who's that for?" I ask.

"It is a card to myself. I write one every year," she says

"Every present needs a card," I say, unconvinced by my own platitude.

"Dear Raga," she reads to me. "Thank you for being so strong and for caring for yourself this year. You have been very brave. Keep treating yourself well. Happy Christmas and Happy New Year! With all my love, Raga."

She closes the card, puts it in the envelope, and hands the envelope to me to put on her present. She could not wrap her own gift, for that would defeat the purpose.

"That is a very powerful message," I say, trying to keep my eyes away by focusing on lining up the next box with the wrapping paper. She is crying. Her wedding ring, which she still wears on her left hand, catches the lamp light as she takes a Kleenex and dabs her eyes. I finish wrapping the new cordless phone she bought for herself, place the card under the ribbon, and the box under the tree.

"That's the last of it," I say. "I think I'll go to bed now. Thank you for a lovely day, Raga."

"Yes, thank you for all your help. Have a good sleep, Sara."

I'm throwing away the scraps of paper in the kitchen when I hear someone moving around in the hall. I hope that it is Kynan, but it is not. It is Duaa. I watch her watch the flickering Chanukah candles. The first night I lit the candles and said the prayers in Hebrew, she asked Kynan's mom if I was practicing a cult ceremony. She had never met a Jewish person before. Now, I am told, she thinks they are beautiful and she stops to watch me light them every night.

I watch from the kitchen as the candles burn out entirely, a small whirlpool of white and blue wax stiffening on the foil. The next night I'll find myself here again, surreptitiously pouring half a bottle of the worst wine I'll ever have down the sink while the flames of six candles extinguish one by one.

Sister
Finalist in the Derick Burleson Poetry Contest

Jane Richards

Anne could knit one heck of a sweater,
pink and purple and teal zig-zags,
a little loose at the neckline;
I own it now,
don it on the coldest days.
I can almost sense her fingers in the weave,
the warm imprint of her body.

There are so few photos of her,
no grave to visit, no urn of ashes,
nor tree planted in her honor,
no memorial service pamphlet--
she wanted none of that.

Instead, she is knitted into my life,
her gifts appearing with regularity:
the butterfly pin from Mexico,
a stained recipe for jelly tots,
the commercial grade measuring spoons,
her advice to avoid buying
those dowdy print dresses.

Her loss defies convention,
refuses to sit in its seat,
stay in the cupboard,
be silent.

So like her.

Sweet Sparrow
Finalist in the Mary Cassatt Art Contest

Jordyn-Elizabeth Pimental

Ebbets Field Bounce
3rd place in the Phil Heldrich Nonfiction Contest

Glenn Moss

If my father had followed his natural strengths, he would have become a high school coach or an instructor at a Fred Astaire studio. Both linked by a rolling grace in his walk, either journey likely would have resulted in a happier man. Instead, perhaps pushed by the macro events of Depression and war, he became a diminished Arthur Miller salesman of women's shoes and a dreamer of deals with other men who found themselves in apartments that were too small and frustrations that grew too large. One way my father tried to maintain connection with his lost self was to have me accompany him on Sunday mornings for games of handball or boxball. Classic games of Brooklyn that allowed him to move and react in ways that bending down to fit a middle-aged woman's foot in a pump did not.

An essential part of this connection was my contribution…to lose and be the non-athletic kid I was told I was, book smart maybe but having "the common sense of a wet rag". My awkward lunges and misses, hitting the ball outside the lines of the designated concrete slab or not hitting the handball with enough force to reach the wall, both defined me and him. My misses were his hits; my losing was his win. For all the consequences that would flow from this, on a Sunday morning in Spring or Fall it was our time and I saw my father differently, diving into himself in a way that left regret in its wake, but the splash of memory let him make it through the week.

How I made it through my week was not a subject of interest. Encased behind my thick black glasses and stutter born from the pressures of regret and anger that broke the words on my tongue, I was the small pot for the family's boil. Each morning, I would walk to school where my sweating inability to speak oiled the friction of others discovery and hormonal twitch. And to be the source of coin, or occasional coat, for the taking. One night, on another solitary walk down Ocean Avenue on early autumn evening, I was relieved of my jacket, and when I made it home a bit scuffed and chilly, nothing was asked or said. When you meet a set of expectations, what is there to say.

One Sunday in 1965 or '66, instead of the Spaldeen or handball, my father picked the basketball. I didn't remember the last time he had and couldn't know then this would be the last. It was a warm July morning and he said we were going over to the Ebbets Field apartments, a housing project representing the quickening changes of the neighborhood. Changes that would soon be wrapped in the term, "white flight", describing the reaction of white middle- and working-class families to the beginnings of poor and working-class Black families moving in. There were a few middle-class Black families, but they had no place to flee to because racism and northern segregation kept them where they were. Whites could find new apartments and homes in Midwood and Sheepshead Bay or Queens and Long Island, but Black families could not. Many of my parent's friends would leave in the next few years, but my parents pretending to be middle-class economically, would be the last.

Ebbets Field, the historic stadium where Jackie Robinson and the Dodgers began to end baseball's segregation. A place representing the hints of the better people we might be and where my father cheered the team, and Jackie too. But the Dodgers left for California and, like almost everyone around him, other changes brought out fears and reactions to those fears. The stadium, torn down by 1960, had been replaced by the Ebbets Field apartments by 1963. Part of the housing project had basketball courts and that's where my father and I headed that morning.

It was early, around 9 AM, and my father probably thought the courts would be empty. He bounced the ball as we walked and talked about Dodgers and Giants, the teams he still followed, and about the upcoming football season. When we crossed Empire Boulevard and approached the project and the courts, they were empty. The gate was open, and we headed to one court, and my father began to do some layups. He would dribble, turn, and pass me the ball, and I would heave it up, clanging it on the rim of the basket.

This went on for about 15 minutes, and then we heard some voices behind us. "Hey man, what you doin' here...this is ours..." Turning, we saw five guys approaching, all looking about 15 or 16. They stopped, just looked, and one came forward and took the basketball from my father's hands, stared at him, started to dribble and passed it to one of the other guys.

The moment of confrontation, challenge and tension extended, my glasses fogged up with sweat and my legs began to shake. My father breathed in deeply and made his decision. He turned to me, said, "Let's go", and we walked towards the gate as the sound of laughter, high fives and a bouncing basketball followed us out.

My father muttered something, I think I heard the word, "element", one of the code words of the time and neighborhood. He told me not to say anything to my mother, he would say we just lost the ball and decided to come home.

We never spoke about it, but I remember thinking something changed or broke in him. It's not that my father had a clear vision for his future; his eyes always seemed to be cast behind. But an extra weight, a thicker layer of cloud entered that day and never left. There were many things that happened in my family we didn't speak about, but this one was something only my father and I shared...and didn't. That morning, I began to realize that we didn't need to speak for my father to teach me lessons both intended and not. How strength and weakness can be confused, how silence can be a grace or a weapon. How being a father is something you need to work at every day. And you still might fail.

My parents never saw it, but those lessons, however buried, weren't forgotten. By the time it was my turn, it took some digging, sweat and cursing to uncover and fully bring them into my light and fatherhood. That walk away from Ebbets Field continues, and there's still dirt to be removed, but my hope is my son can carry some of these lessons with him. He has other things to dig for, different lessons from an imperfect dad, but at least they'll be his and not buried so deep.

Where Dreams Take Place
Finalist in the Derick Burleson Poetry Contest

Andrea Reynolds

Though I'm nearly 100 years old,
most of my dreams
take place in my childhood
flat. It doesn't matter
the premise.

Last night, I was 75
bickering with my skinny husband
over watering the lawn, but I
was in my 7-year-old bedroom.
Bright wallpaper with petals
shaped like teardrops spinning
pink and orange.

Tiny lime green tiles flew
off of the fireplace.
The hairline crack in the plaster
edged toward my sister's bed.
And I was yelling, *Stop
watering the grass.*

Halfway to the Peak
Finalist in the Mary Cassatt Art Contest

Jordyn-Elizabeth Pimental

Malneirophrenia
1st Place in the Susan Hansell Drama Contest

One-Act Play
Brian C. Billings

CHARACTERS
    APHRODITE, the goddess of love (in voice only)
    EROS, the god of desire and husband to PSYCHE
    HYPNOS, the god of sleep
    THE ONEIROI, the sons of HYPNOS (all in one body)
        MORPHEUS, bringer of dreams of humans
        PHANTASOS, bringer of dreams of the inanimate
        PHOBETOR, bringer of dreams of animals
    PSYCHE, the most beautiful woman in the world and wife to EROS

TIME AND PLACE
    The action takes place in Hypnos's grotto in Erebos, the place of eternal darkness, deep in the Underworld.

(Dim, golden light rises to reveal the grotto of HYPNOS. The light spills from six inverted torches bracketed evenly along the US wall. Water diverted from the nearby River Lethe trickles through channels carved in the rough stone. Columns hollowed out with alcoves stretch to the ceiling at either end of the room. Each column contains multiple shelves stuffed with leather-cased scrolls. Three S-shaped lounging couches with grey-and-gold cushions rest at CS, CSR, and CSL. HYPNOS, dressed in a pigeon-grey tunic and ochre sandals, perches on the edge of the CSR couch while perusing an unrolled scroll on his lap. A pot of ink rests to his left, and he taps a bronze stylus absently against the eagle wings that sprout from his head. EROS enters at SL as the epitome of weariness. His normally white tunic is blotched with stains. His wings droop, and HE drags his bow and quiver of arrows behind him. Even the straps securing his sandals to his calves are loose.)

HYPNOS

Late again, Eros. I've been waiting nearly twenty minutes. Wings and weapons at the door, please.

(EROS drops his bow and quiver to the ground. HE pulls a clasp at his left shoulder, and his wings slide off his shoulders into a fluffy heap. HE shuffles to the CS couch and flops down on his back with a groan.)

                              EROS
I can't sleep. It's been *months.*

                            HYPNOS
You were just here last week.

                              EROS
Well, it's been months in mortal time, and I spend more time there than here.

                            HYPNOS
I hope you haven't been overexerting yourself.

        (HE sets aside the scroll.)

                              EROS
If only. I don't have the focus for that. There's a man in Thrace who's madly in love
with his dinner because I took a bad shot.

                            HYPNOS
Maybe he'll become an epicurean.

                              EROS
Optimist.

                            HYPNOS
A misfire isn't necessarily a mistake. Recall, if you will, the affair of the lizard, the rock,
and the arrow. The results have been quite popular.

                              EROS
I suppose. I'm told there's good eating on a turtle.

                            HYPNOS
Especially in soup...which is where you seem to find yourself these days.

                              EROS
Nights, Hypnos. Days I can deal with.

                            HYPNOS
No improvement at all?

                              EROS
None.

        (HYPNOS reclaims his scroll. HE dips his stylus in the ink and begins taking notes
        while HE talks.)

HYPNOS

Let's check the symptoms just to be certain. Tossing and turning.

EROS

More like thrashing and rolling. Poseidon could take lessons.

HYPNOS

Delayed reaction time.

EROS

I crashed into Mother's statue over in Athens.

HYPNOS

Blurry vision, I assume.

EROS

How else can you fail to see a sculpture forty feet high? I think I knocked an arm off.

HYPNOS

Oh, that happens all the time.

EROS

Tell that to Mother.

HYPNOS

I enjoy my existence, thank you. Lack of appetite?

EROS

I can manage maybe half a cup of ambrosia. Any more than that sits like a stone in my stomach. Mostly I've been having warm nectar before bedtime.

HYPNOS

Snacks aren't meals.

EROS

I'm doing the best I can!

HYPNOS

And there's the last one: irritability. Breathe, Eros.

(EROS takes a breath, holds it for a four-count, and exhales.)

EROS

I can't get her out of my mind, Hypnos.

                                    HYPNOS
By *her* you mean Psyche.

                                     EROS
I need her. She's my wife!

                                    HYPNOS
We've talked about this. She burned you, Eros. Badly.

                                     EROS
I shouldn't have stormed out on her.

                                    HYPNOS
You were hurt.

                                     EROS
I was confused! I woke up with a face full of hot wax, and there she was poking a candle
in my eyes. I panicked! I needed to get away!

                                    HYPNOS
So flighty.

                                     EROS
Mother says that, too.

                                    HYPNOS
She also told you Psyche left.

                                     EROS
I would feel that. I would know! I keep thinking I hear her voice …especially at night. I
reach out expecting to find her sleeping by my side, but every time there's only air.
Someone's taken her. One of the other gods, probably. Maybe Hades. He's done that
kind of thing before.

                                    HYPNOS
He wouldn't. He's happy with Persephone.

                                     EROS
Then why can't I find her? She's not in the Heavens. She's nowhere on Earth. I had
Charon check the ferry manifest, and she hasn't crossed into the Underworld. I hope
you'd say something if you'd seen her.

                                    HYPNOS
I would.

EROS

Then I have to keep looking. We might be dealing with metamorphosis or some kind of sealing. She wouldn't be the first girl trapped in a tree.

HYPNOS

Nor the last, I think, but let's help you find some way to rest before you dig up the countryside.

EROS

I can't afford the delay!

HYPNOS

Yet here you are keeping our usual appointment.

EROS

Out of habit. And …you seem like you care.

HYPNOS

Then trust me when I say that closing your eyes now will help you see better later.

 (HE scribbles some final thoughts and traces the Greek symbol for air over the scroll. An echoing chime sounds. HE tests the now-dry ink with a finger and nods with satisfaction. HE rolls up his notes and sets the stylus behind an ear.)

I want to try a different technique. Tell me about your dreams.

EROS

I can't sleep! Remember?

HYPNOS

Even the worst insomniac drops off upon occasion. Call it a microsleep. You wouldn't even register the blackout, but a dream can live in a handful of seconds.

EROS

Then I don't dream.

HYPNOS

More likely you don't remember the dreams.

 (HE calls off SR.)

Morpheus!

 (A young god enters. MORPHEUS' clothes perfectly duplicate HYPNOS's raiment, but his tunic is chalked with abstract shapes. MORPHEUS wears a half-mask with wolf ears and black fur. Two other half-masks hang from a belt at his waist: one framed in small gems and one with hyper-extended black eyes. MORPHEUS growls when HE spots EROS.)

HYPNOS (CONT.)

Oh. Phobetor. I didn't realize you were dominant. I want to talk to Morpheus. Bring him out, won't you?

(The young man ducks his head. HE removes his mask, places it on his belt, and puts on the large-eyed mask to become MORPHEUS.)

MORPHEUS

Father. Will you need me long? Phobetor was herding the golden sheep for tonight's counting.

HYPNOS

He can do his woolgathering later. I need your help with a client.

MORPHEUS

Waking or sleeping?

HYPNOS

Waking. Tell me how often Eros has been dreaming.

(MORPHEUS crosses to EROS. MORPHEUS kneels behind the god and places his fingers lightly on EROS's temples. EROS flinches.)

EROS

Cold hands!

MORPHEUS

Small wonder. I dwell at length among the dark recesses of the mind.

EROS

And now I'm terrified.

HYPNOS

You're in good hands.

EROS

But can I get out of them?

HYPNOS

Don't worry. He's harmless, and we only need a moment.

(MORPHEUS releases EROS and rises.)

MORPHEUS

He dreams constantly, Father, but strangely. The same visions rise and fall and return without change.

HYPNOS

No wonder he's exhausted. He's been running a marathon. Can you tell me why?

MORPHEUS

I can sense patterns repeating, but a veil clouds the details.

HYPNOS

You're the god of dreams. There shouldn't be a problem.

MORPHEUS

Agreed. I find the experience...frustrating. I suggest a projection.

HYPNOS

Excellent idea! Find a kylix and bring over some water.

>   (MORPHEUS crosses to the column at SL and removes a wide-bowled drinking cup from one of the alcoves. EROS jerks upright in alarm.)

EROS

Excuse me! I'm not sure I *want* a projection.

>   (MORPHEUS moves over to the wall and collects Lethe water in the cup.)

HYPNOS

Perhaps *projection* has the wrong flavor. *Construction* describes the procedure better, I think. Working from sensation, my sons and I will build what we find in your dreams layer by layer. Phantasos will set the scene, Phobetor will populate it, and Morpheus will animate it.

>   (MORPHEUS returns to EROS's side and offers him the cup.)

Once we can see what's been causing you distress, you can confront it and banish it. Drink the water, please.

EROS

That's water from the Lethe! I want my wits to stay where they are.

HYPNOS

The water's *filtered*, and I was about to bestow a blessing anyway.

>   (HE traces the Greek symbol for water over the cup. A rippling chime sounds.)

HYPNOS, Cont.

You'll only forget your anxieties. I swear. We can't build a proper construct if you're fussing like a wet sphinx.

  (MORPHEUS presses the cup closer to EROS.)

EROS

I'll be able to sleep afterwards?

HYPNOS

Deeper than Endymion.

MORPHEUS

We think.

HYPNOS

The odds are good.

MORPHEUS

Even at the least.

EROS

Well, why not? Nothing else has helped.

  (HE takes the cup and drinks from it lightly. MORPHEUS takes the cup and places it on the ground near the edge of the couch.)

HYPNOS

Now repeat the mantra I taught you a few weeks ago.

EROS

A grand Greek god gives grace to good Greeks.

HYPNOS

Slower.

EROS

A grand...Greek god gives...grace to good...Greeks.

HYPNOS

Slower!

EROS

A grand...Greek god...gives...grace...to...

(The torchlight begins pulsing in a slow rhythm. EROS relaxes completely. HE stares into a misty distance. MORPHEUS crosses to him and runs his hands over and around EROS's head.)

MORPHEUS

He lies entranced, Father. Phantasos can begin now.

(MORPHEUS ducks his head and swaps his mask with the begemmed mask. PHANTASOS moves his arms in a slow, cyclical fashion. Lights dim in the main area even as they rise DSL on a freestanding screen. Mounds of grains and seeds— barley, corn, millet, poppies, and wheat—appear on the screen in projection. A barefooted PSYCHE, clad in an elaborately pinned tunic of purple and yellow, walks out from behind the screen. SHE carries an urn filled with more grains and seeds. SHE looks as weary as EROS. Even so, SHE remains eerily beautiful. PHANTASOS swaps masks to become PHOBETOR, who scratches at the air. Small dots of light appear around PSYCHE's feet. PHOBETOR swaps masks to become MORPHEUS, who forms a triangle with his fingers. The dots of light begin marching. PSYCHE speaks, but EROS provides her voice.)

PSYCHE

Here are the grains and the seeds I have gathered in order to satisfy
What you demand. In this urn are the best from the dunes I have
Piled in the hopes they will please you and finally finish my sifting through
Plants from the harvest. Although I am tired, if you find any fault in the
Gifts that I bring, I will gladly begin with my sifting again. Are you
Pleased with my work, Aphrodite so fair? Does the grist of the crop on the
Ground make you smile? Though I may have been helped by industrious
Ants who were moved by my plight, I was never at rest. They were merely a
Means by which sorting came faster. They guided my hands into mastery.

(Red light flashes angrily. The projected mounds shake and dissolve. PSYCHE flails around in the grip of a small earthquake. APHRODITE's voice sneers at her from offstage.)

APHRODITE

Gather the grains! Your ordeal is not over! Your helpers have ruined you!

(PSYCHE vanishes in a blackout. Lights rise to normal in the main area. ORPHEUS shakes out his fingers as if they've been stung. EROS begins thrashing on the couch. HYPNOS holds him down.)

EROS

Psyche! Psyche!

HYPNOS

Morpheus! More water!

(HYPNOS waves an arm, and the torchlight stops pulsing. MORPHEUS scoops
up the kylix and forces a drink past EROS's lips. After a beat, EROS relaxes.)

MORPHEUS
Aphrodite's in his dreams, Father.

(HE sets the cup back on the ground. HYPNOS begins pacing.)

HYPNOS
No, no. Just her voice. She can't push in much more than that. She'd be trespassing on
your territory. But Psyche's really there! She's not a construct. Aphrodite's trapped her
in her husband's dreams. No wonder he couldn't find her.

MORPHEUS
My realm is preternatural. Should she remain there, her substance will erode.

HYPNOS
That's the point. Aphrodite can kill Psyche and torture her son at the same time ...and
nobody would have known if Eros hadn't come in for counseling. Clever.

MORPHEUS
Why torture him?

HYPNOS
For loving Psyche. Keep up, son! Classic overprotectiveness. Or jealousy. Either way,
she's a wonderfully nasty mother, isn't she?

MORPHEUS
Eros is helping. The ants arise from sympathetic intuition.

HYPNOS
True, but the dream keeps repeating.

MORPHEUS
Which makes him feel like he's failing her.

HYPNOS
Which means?

MORPHEUS
He can't sleep.

HYPNOS
You make me so proud sometimes! Can you pull Psyche out of there?

MORPHEUS

I'll need to study the dream for cracks.

HYPNOS

Then we should press on. Eros, can you hear me?

EROS

Mother?

HYPNOS

Thankfully not. Use your words, Eros. A grand Greek god…

EROS

…gives grace to good Greeks.

  (HYPNOS waves a hand in a circle. The torchlight begins pulsing once more.)

HYPNOS

A greater Greek god…

EROS

….gives grateful Greeks grandeur.

HYPNOS

Again.

  (EROS recites, and his words slowly fade out. MORPHEUS swaps masks and becomes PHANTASOS, who begins conjuring the dream. Lights fade in the main area and rise on the DSL screen. The projection is now the River Estige's ferocious waterfall. Jagged rocks stick out of the dark water like spears. PSYCHE, holding a stoppered amphora, steps out from behind the screen. SHE is drenched. PHANTASOS swaps masks to become PHOBETOR, who spreads out his fingers and shakes them. The outline of an eagle appears on one of the rocks. PHOBETOR swaps masks to become MORPHEUS, who gives the scene life. The eagle-shape begins flapping its wings in a stop-motion fashion. PSYCHE holds out the amphora and speaks in EROS's voice.)

PSYCHE

Water you wanted, and water I have. \My amphora contains more than
What you might want. Though the water descending so swiftly was strong, I was
Brave as I stepped on the slippery stones. With a single misstep I would
Surely have shattered my body and perished at once. It's a blessing an
Eagle was passing and pitied my efforts at catching the drops of the
Estige's flood. On a swoop through the spray he took off with my vessel, and
Then he returned with my amphora filled. He was even so kind as to

Guide me to safety. Without his indulgence I doubt I'd have managed the
Path to the bank. Now my task is complete. You can set me at liberty.

(APHRODITE's voice rises offstage.)

APHRODITE
When will you learn? These assignments are never for others' completion.
Liberty. When have I shackled you? Do as I say and my Eros will
Fly to your side. You agreed that my tasks would provide me with proof that your
Love was sincere. Is a little assurance too much for a mother to
Ask? Will you act on your own? If you won't, then my son should be rid of you.

(PSYCHE turns back to the waterfall in resignation. A spotlight rises on
MORPHEUS. HE cries out and reaches for her.)

MORPHEUS
Psyche, your hand! You are trapped in a vision! Your husband is here with me!
Though you've not heard me before, I am Morpheus, shaper of fantasy.
Hypnos, my father, attends you as well at the height of your misery.

APHRODITE
Silence, you godling! Although you are Lord of the Dreams, my command of the
Bond that evolves out of love is a power you can't dissipate though you
Strike it with force or with words. If you only will wait, she will atrophy.
Silence will reign in your realm, and I swear to depart with alacrity.

MORPHEUS
Psyche, again I appeal! Will you give me your hand? I can… . That is …

(APHRODITE laughs as MORPHEUS fumbles for words. Red light flashes, and
PSYCHE fades from view. MORPHEUS's spotlight falls as the main lighting
reasserts itself. HE snaps his fingers in frustration. HYPNOS draws the Greek
symbol for earth and holds out his hands to either side of the symbol. A cymbal
crash erupts and fades. The torches pulse faster.)

HYPNOS
We need to return! We nearly had her!

MORPHEUS
I'm sorry, Father. Dactylic hexameter is difficult!

(HYPNOS's hands begin to shake.)

HYPNOS
Save the apologia for later. I can't preserve the link for long.

(EROS sits up. HE remains entranced.)

EROS

Give her back, Mother! I'll bring you sparrows and swans! Myrtles and roses!

HYPNOS

He's waking up!

EROS

Your vanity is killing us!

 (MORPHEUS scoops the kylix off the floor and splashes the last of the water into
 EROS's face. EROS drops to the couch unconscious. MORPHEUS places his
 brothers' masks over his own. HE crosses to HYPNOS and spreads out his arms.
 HE and HYPNOS make a pushing motion together. Lights drop on them as a harsh
 spotlight rises on PSYCHE at DSL. SHE stands in front of the screen, which is
 blank and dark. Her clothes are dry, her hair is styled, and SHE wears golden
 sandals. SHE holds a small wooden box close to her chest. SHE speaks, but this
 time SHE uses her own voice.)

PSYCHE

Over and over I've slaved in your trials believing my labors were
Proving my worth. Now I learn you've misled me and all of my effort was
Fuel for your cruelty. Never again will I heed your commands! You've a
Reckoning coming with ultimate prejudice. Psyche the servant no
Longer obeys you. She brings you instead her own means of escaping.
Here is the box with Persephone's beauty you bade me to beg from the
Queen of the Dead. If I swallow the contents to aid my attraction then
Surely my charms will expand in degree so that even a goddess will
Fail to compare. I dismiss you! My beauty delivers your banishment!

 (SHE opens the box and consumes what lies within. SHE drops the box to the
 ground and kneels. A furiously bright kaleidoscope of color bathes her.
 APHRODITE shrieks. PSYCHE vanishes in a blackout. Lights immediately rise in
 HYPNOS's chamber. The torches are still. PSYCHE now kneels directly in front of
 HYPNOS and MORPHEUS, who lean upon each other. THEY separate as PSYCHE
 rises, and HYPNOS guides her to EROS. MORPHEUS removes his layered masks.
 HE wobbles and switches into PHOBETOR to regain some primal strength. HE
 crosses to PSYCHE's side. SHE sits on the couch and takes EROS's head in her lap.
 HE stirs and tries to rise.)

EROS

Found you.

(PSYCHE pulls him back down.)

PSYCHE

You did. Don't leave me again.

EROS

Never!

PSYCHE

Then sleep.

(SHE turns down his eyelids, and EROS sleeps.)

Thank you, Hypnos. And thanks to you, too, Morpheus.

(PHOBETOR whines.)

HYPNOS

I'm afraid that's Phobetor. Morpheus couldn't hold on any longer.

PSYCHE

I understand.

(SHE scratches PHOBETOR between the ears.)

Good boy.

(HE pants happily.)

HYPNOS

You two should be safe in the grotto.

PSYCHE

We can deal with Aphrodite.

HYPNOS

Boldly stated, but, actually, you can't. She's hardly Hestia. Besides, she's made this a godly matter now. Let me talk to Zeus. He has his ways of sorting out his daughter. He usually enjoys it.

(HE crosses to the SL entrance.)

Come along, son. We need to find our fancy tunics. And maybe some pears. Hera likes those, doesn't she?

(HYPNOS exits. After another head-scratch from PSYCHE, PHOBETOR follows his father. PSYCHE lies down with her husband. PHOBETOR stops at the exit and becomes PHANTASOS. HE makes the Greek symbol for fire, which prompts a muted whoomp. The torches begin dying out. HE exits. Blackout.)

Nightwalking
Finalist in the Derick Burleson Poetry Contest

Frank William Finney

Tears crawl
like spiders—

webs for the face.

A dreary walk
in a dreary town—

Nobody else near
to see or hear

the circling bats;
the owls in my head.

And yet there's solace
in the streetlights' haze—

And mine
the only footfall.

Silhouettes at Sundown
Finalist in the Mary Cassatt Art Contest

Karen Colstrom

Lost
2nd Place in the Susan Hansell Drama Contest

Sherrie Pesta

This One Act is comprised of three scenes. The staging should be simple, symbolic.

CHARACTERS *(In Order of Appearance)*
	ELDERLY MAN (M, 65+)
	YOUNG MAN (M, 20-25)
	YOUNG LADY (F, 19-25)
	YOUNG GIRL (F, 8-10)
	WOMAN (F, 35-45)
	EMT (E)
	DISGRUNTLED (M, 25-35)
	SARCASTIC (F, 25-35)
	BEWILDERED (M, 25-35)
	CUNNING (E, 40-55)

SCENE ONE: In a Park

(A Saturday morning. One bench sits UC. When lights rise, an ELDERLY MAN slumps on the bench, his eyes closed. There's a stack of 'Lost Cat' fliers beside him. He has stuck one of the fliers to the arm of the bench, where the audience can see it.)

(YOUNG MAN enters SR, running to catch a ball. He exits SL after it. YOUNG LADY and YOUNG GIRL enter SR.)

YOUNG LADY

I know what you're doing.

YOUNG GIRL

I doubt it.

YOUNG LADY

Quit making him chase that ball! He's not a dog.

YOUNG GIRL

A dog would be more fun.

YOUNG LADY

Please, don't ruin this for me.

YOUNG GIRL

You said we'd go shopping today.

YOUNG LADY

We can go tomorrow. We have the whole weekend.

YOUNG GIRL

But Lavender Bear goes on sale *today*.

(Sees ELDERLY MAN on bench and points.)

Who's that?

YOUNG LADY

(Turns, startled)

My god! Is he asleep?

(GIRL crosses to MAN and extends hand.)

Don't touch him!

(YOUNG MAN enters SL with ball.)

YOUNG MAN

Good throw, kid!

(Seeing her over the ELDERLY MAN)

Is that man dead?

(YOUNG GIRL shrieks and YOUNG LADY pulls her in. YOUNG MAN drops ball and crosses UC.)

YOUNG LADY

Hold something over his face. See if he's breathing.

(YOUNG MAN wiggles a flier out from pile and holds it in front of ELDERLY MAN's face. Nothing. YOUNG GIRL reads flier.)

YOUNG GIRL

"Lost Cat"!

(YOUNG GIRL takes the flier from YOUNG MAN.)

That's so sad. He must be looking for her.

YOUNG MAN

Or was.

(YOUNG MAN whispers.)

Not sure he's breathing.

(Pause)

Should we call the police?

YOUNG LADY

(Whispering)

That could take all day. They'll question us! We're not supposed to be in a park. I'll get fired!

YOUNG MAN

Calm down.

YOUNG LADY

I should not be here with you. I should have taken her shopping like I promised.

YOUNG GIRL

(Having heard the whispering)

That's what I said.

YOUNG MAN

(Speaking full voice)

I can't just leave this man here.

(Pause. No response.)

You two can leave.

(YOUNG LADY begins to pull YOUNG GIRL out SR. YOUNG GIRL breaks free and returns to bench.)

YOUNG GIRL

(Scooping up a stack of fliers)

We should put up some of his fliers.

YOUNG LADY

If he's (gesturing weakly towards Elderly Man) ... dead..., he's not going to miss a cat.

(YOUNG GIRL scowls at YOUNG LADY, who continues.)

And...if we find the cat...with him being...dead...what then?

YOUNG GIRL

I keep it!

(She runs off SR.)

YOUNG LADY

I am so fired.

(She exits SR.)

YOUNG MAN
(Dialing cell phone)

Yes, I...there's an emergency... . I'm...in Seven Hills Park. ...Near the soccer fields.... There's an Elderly Man on a bench... . What? No, he doesn't appear hurt. ...But he doesn't seem alive either. ...I said alive. I mean... mybe *not* alive?

WOMAN
(Entering SR in a hurry and seeing ELDERLY MAN)

Dad! Thank goodness.

(She hurries over and hugs him. He slouches over onto bench.)

Oh, no.

YOUNG MAN
(Continuing into phone)

...Probably dead. You should send someone. ... Near the 4th street entrance.

(Having pushed ELDERLY MAN back up, WOMAN sits. She holds MAN while searching purse. YOUNG MAN hangs up.)

WOMAN

He's not dead. He's diabetic.

(She finds a shot and shoves it into leg.)

                    ELDERLY MAN
          (Fluttering eyes towards Woman)

Maggie? …. Maggie ….

                    WOMAN
          (Wrapping an arm around his shoulders).

Sshh…

          (He sinks into her, eyes closed again, as she speaks softly to him.)

Quit wandering off alone. You worry me.

                    YOUNG MAN
Your name is Maggie?

                    WOMAN
          (Without looking up from ELDERLY MAN) No.

                    YOUNG MAN
(Pause) The cat then.

          (She looks at him confused.)

The flier. He's looking for his cat.

                    WOMAN
The cat … *is* dead. (Pause) Died over a year ago.

                    YOUNG MAN
He doesn't know?

                    WOMAN
Alzheimer's. …

                    YOUNG MAN
Alzheimer's *and* Diabetes?

                    WOMAN
Getting old sucks. …

          (Sounds of an ambulance arriving)

Did I hear you call 9-1-1?

                    YOUNG MAN
Yes?

                     WOMAN
I can't afford another ambulance. Help me get him to my car.

                    YOUNG MAN
          (Backing up)

I don't know....

                     WOMAN
Fine. I'll do it myself.

          (She shifts ELDERLY MAN down and talks to him.)

Right back.

          (She exits SL.)

                    YOUNG MAN
WHERE ARE YOU ...?

          (He paces nervously. He decides to cross UC and examine ELDERLY MAN. He lifts
          ELDERLY MAN and leans him back up on bench. EMT enters SL.)

                      EMT
Avoid touching the patient, please!

          (YOUNG MAN releases and the ELDERLY MAN slides down face first. EMT rushes
          to bench.)

                      EMT
Are you this man's son?

          (YOUNG MAN shakes head 'no'.)

Grandson?

          (YOUNG MAN shakes head 'no'.)

Then who...?

                    YOUNG MAN
... I called 9-1-1.

                                    EMT

So, you found him.

         (YOUNG MAN is struck by the words.)

Alone?

                                 YOUNG MAN

No... I was with a ... friend ... and her ...

                                    EMT

Not you. Him. Was HE alone?

         (WOMAN enters SR with a cane. Stops out of sight; motions to YOUNG MAN to
         keep her out of it.)

                                 YOUNG MAN

No ... I mean ... Yes? ... I ... cannot say ... that I saw someone *with* him.

         (As the EMT stares, ELDERLY MAN wakes.)

                                ELDERLY MAN

(To EMT) Who the HELL are you? (Grabbing up fliers*)* MAGGIE?

                                 YOUNG MAN

He seems fine now. Maybe you could just let him go home.

                                    EMT

With whom? ... Who's Maggie? ... (Pause.) You're not related to him? (Pause) ... Listen,
we need to check him out. If he's 'fine,' and *someone* wants to take him home...we will
consider releasing him into a *relative's* custody.

         EMT guides ELDERLY MAN off SL. WOMAN enters SR and storms up to YOUNG
         MAN.)

                                   WOMAN

Why do you have to be involved? You don't have your own problems to solve?

                                 YOUNG MAN

I thought you didn't want to pay for an ambulance.

                                   WOMAN

(Pause. Almost tearful) I'm *not* a terrible daughter.

                                 YOUNG MAN

Of course not. ... I didn't say you were. (Pause) It must be really ... difficult to ...

                                WOMAN
(Exiting SL hurriedly) Thank you. DAD! Wait!

                              YOUNG GIRL
(Entering SR) Where's the old guy?

                              YOUNG MAN
Gone.

                              YOUNG GIRL
Lost?

                              YOUNG MAN
You might say that.

                              YOUNG GIRL
We got lost, too!

                              YOUNG MAN
What do you mean? Where's ....?

                              YOUNG LADY
(Entering SR, exhausted) We got confused putting up fliers in these woods.

                              YOUNG GIRL
(Full of happy energy*)* Then we heard an ambulance!

        (YOUNG MAN points out SL and YOUNG GIRL runs off. YOUNG LADY starts to
        exit, but YOUNG MAN stops her.)

                              YOUNG MAN
Let her go. You can see her from here.

                              YOUNG LADY
She could get hurt.

                              YOUNG MAN
What could happen with an EMT standing right beside her?

        (He reaches for one of her hands.)

                              YOUNG LADY
(Slipping past him to cross to the remaining fliers on the ground)

Help me throw these away. I'm not hanging any more fliers today.

YOUNG MAN
(Taking the fliers from her gently and holding her hand)

You don't have to. The cat's not lost.

YOUNG LADY

Thank goodness!

YOUNG MAN

The cat's dead.

YOUNG LADY
(Overwhelmed) NO! (Panicking) Not the man, too?

YOUNG MAN

Might as well be.

YOUNG LADY
(Pause. Looking pale and exhausted.)

I feel so … helpless.
YOUNG MAN
(Pause. He gazes at her.)

Let's start over. Go somewhere less … whatever this is. … Tomorrow?

YOUNG LADY
(Tired) I will be with munchkin all day. If I disappear, try searching Build-a-Bear.

YOUNG MAN
Next Saturday, then. Next Saturday *Night*. We could see a movie.

YOUNG LADY
(Pause) Sure.

(They begin walking to exit SL.)

What could go wrong?

(Lights down.)

Scene Two: In a Break Room
(Monday. It's lunch hour in a chain store break room. Several aluminum chairs surround a card table, DSR/DC. An easel holds a bulletin board, DL. On the board hang a work duty schedule, sign-up sheets for intramural teams, and a "Lost Cat" flier. A small table UC holds a coffee pot and cups. When lights rise,

DISGRUNTLED and SARCASTIC are unpacking their lunches. They wear sweaters.)

DISGRUNTLED

That's the second store lock-down in a week. If parents just kept an eye on their children, they wouldn't get lost.

SARCASTIC

Now why blame the parents? No one is perfect. So, they let their little ones play tag through the lingerie or hide-and-seek around the lawnmowers. How should they know the dangers involved?

DISGRUNTLED

I'm not here to babysit someone else's poor decision. (Counting out chips). They come in here with not one...not two... but a minivan full. They're not likely to notice at first if a single toddler (eats a chip) goes missing.

(BEWILDERED enters breakroom. Looks around. He wears a tie and a Manager pin. Heads to coffee.)

SARCASTIC

Speaking of lost....

(BEWILDERED wanders to their table and sits.)

DISGRUNTLED

The manager's break room is down the hall two doors.

BEWILDERED

(Without moving) Yes.

SARCASTIC

I could draw you a map.

BEWILDERED

No need. I prefer it here.

DISGRUNTLED

Sure. Why choose a newly remodeled lounge with baskets of fresh fruit and a cappuccino machine when you can have all...this.

SARCASTIC

(Admiring DISGRUNTLED) Wow! I'm rubbing off on you.

BEWILDERED

Have you ever stopped and wondered..., "What am I doing with my life? How did I get here?"

DISGRUNTLED and SARCASTIC
Every Morning.   Every Second.
With every dismal Customer.   With every whining Clown.
Why do you ask?

BEWILDERED
(Standing and crossing to easel board.)

I thought this job would be fun. Talking with people … who shop. … I like talking … and shopping.

DISGRUNTLED and SARCASTIC
Uh-huh.

BEWILDERED
But it's boring. Tedious.

DISGRUNTLED
I've been working here over six years. Key word: WORK, *not* 'Fun'.

SARCASTIC
(To DISGRUNTLED) But, my friend, you're a clerk. WE are lowly servants to the masses. THIS man is a MANAGER! Surely, he can expect more FUN out of his time here than we can.

BEWILDERED
Wouldn't you think so! It's all spread sheets, and phone calls. And now I've been put in charge of …

(Looks around before saying in a loud whisper)

… layoffs!

DISGRUNTLED
Layoffs?

BEWILDERED
Something about making the budget tighter …. Releasing 20%, the 'dead weight'.

(He looks at the schedules posted on the board.)

I guess I could just randomly pick names.

SARCASTIC
(Standing angrily) And I could just randomly poison a cappuccino machine!

(DISGRUNTLED pulls on SARCASTIC's sweater.)

DISGRUNTLED

Perhaps the two of us could aid you in some way? We could … share insider secrets.

SARCASTIC

Of course! We know all the gossip. From who drinks in the dressing rooms to who takes one piece out of every puzzle box just for kicks.

DISGRUNTLED
(Pointing to a name on the sign in sheet)

Thomas here totes his teacup poodle around in a fanny pack while stocking groceries.

BEWILDERED

Is that hygienic?

SARCASTIC
(Pointing to another name)

And Bethany. She's supposed to be selling baby clothes, so why is she always circling through Cosmetics?

BEWILDERED

She probably gets turned around. It's understandable in a store this enormous.

SARCASTIC

Let's just say someone should do a surprise inventory of the nail polish aisle.

BEWILDERED
(It takes a moment to register.)

One of our employees is a thief?

SARCASTIC

You said it, not me.

CUNNING

(Entering unnoticed) There you are! Did you mistake …. Is it *freezing* in this cubicle?

DISGRUNTLED and SARCASTIC
Always.

CUNNING
(Ignoring them. To BEWILDERED)

What are you doing in here?

                    BEWILDERED
Talking with these two ....

                     CUNNING
Interviewing the employees. Fascinating approach.

                    BEWILDERED
I've been thinking, sir....

                     CUNNING
That's not what we pay you for.

                    BEWILDERED
That's just it. What is my purpose here? I'm not feeling I ... fit in.

                     CUNNING
But you CAN fit in. Here at Winkles, we like to think of ourselves as one big happy
TEAM. Us against the world – against our major competitors anyway.

        (Pointing to the intramural sign-up sheets, CUNNING continues.)

Can we count on you to help BEAT the competition?
                    BEWILDERED
You want me to join the ...

        (squinting at what Cunning seems to be pointing at)

Pickleball team?

                     CUNNING
What sport are you best at? We need WINNERS!

                    BEWILDERED
I suppose ... baseball?

                     CUNNING
Wonderful!

                    DISGRUNTLED
        (Packing up lunch and standing)

I best get back to finding kidnapped children.

                     CUNNING
It just so happens our intramural Softball team needs a shortstop.

BEWILDERED

I was a shortstop on my minor league baseball team, the Wasps! What a crazy coincidence!

SARCASTIC

Shocking.

CUNNING

You start next Saturday. A winning season could mean a promotion for ALL!

(DISGRUNTLED and SARCASTIC stop, hearing a glimmer of hope.)

All *Players*, that is.

SARCASTIC
(Standing to exit with DISGRUNTLED.)

While I'm allowed to work double shifts through the games, no doubt.

(Cunning looks at SARCASTIC. She pivots.)

Yay!

CUNNING
(Eyes on SARCASTIC and DISGRUNTLED, to BEWILDERED.)

Have you started that Layoff list?

SARCASTIC	DISGRUNTLED
Gotta fly!	Customers waiting!

(They rush towards the exit.)

CUNNING
(See's "Lost Cat" poster). What's this doing on the employee board?

DISGRUNTLED

A young girl brought it in. Hoped someone might see the cat.

CUNNING
(Ripping it down) If the girl comes back, sell her a stuffed one.

(Lights down.)

Scene 3: At the Movies

Next Saturday Night, in the Lobby of a Movie Complex. Off SR is Entrance and Concessions. UR is the frame of a door with a curtain pulled aside – the entrance to Theater I, showing an R-rated movie. UL is another door frame with a curtain pulled aside – entrance to Theater II, showing a G-rated movie. SL exits to the bathrooms. As lights rise, DISGRUNTLED and SARCASTIC stand C wearing movie uniforms.

DISGRUNTLED

I can't believe he sacked me!

SARCASTIC

I can.

DISGRUNTLED

At least he sacked you, too.

SARCASTIC

Harder to believe. I'm such a charmer.

DISGRUNTLED

Back to minimum wage. How am I to keep up my lifestyle working 20 hours a week in a teenager's job?

SARCASTIC

Fair concern. Fast food prices are on the rise.

DISGRUNTLED

I suppose you shop organic.

SARCASTIC

Only for my kitten, Zeus. I can exist on canned peas and smoothies myself.

(WOMAN and ELDERLY MAN enter SR. Cross C.)

ELDERLY MAN

What movie are we seeing?

WOMAN

I just told you. We're seeing an animated film. *The Forest Guides*.

ELDERLY MAN

Sounds boring.

DISGRUNTLED

(Tearing tickets and pointing UL) *The Forest Guides* will be in Theater II. Watch your step.

ELDERLY MAN

What's playing in Theater I?

SARCASTIC

Evil Lurks Around the Corner

WOMAN

The title alone gives me shivers.

ELDERLY MAN

Docsn't sound boring at least.

WOMAN

(Dragging him UL) Come on, old man. You'll be the death of me.

(WOMAN and ELDERLY MAN exit UL, to Movie II.)

SARCASTIC

Best not tempt fate.

(CUNNING enters SR with a large drink. Crosses C.)

SARCASTIC

(Tearing his tickets with a glare) *Evil Lurks Around the Corner* in Theater I.

CUNNING

There's something lurking … around a corner?

DISGRUNTLED

(Impatiently and angrily pointing UR) Your MOVIE, Evil. Lurks. Around. The. Corner. is *playing* in Theater I.

CUNNING

Ah! (Starts to exit but stops and stares.) You two look familiar. (Pause) No. Never mind. (Exits UR).

(BEWILDERED and YOUNG GIRL enter SR and cross C. She has candy and a Lavender Bear.)

BEWILDERED

(Naively) Hey! I didn't see you guys at the game today! I looked for you in the bleachers, but there were so many faces yours could easily have been lost in the crowd.

DISGRUNTLED

(Flatly) Cheered on by the masses, were you?

YOUNG GIRL
Dad was a Hero! He won the game for Winkles.

SARCASTIC
(Shortly) No doubt.

(YOUNG GIRL crosses L. BEWILDERED watches her. She hangs a Cat Flier near the bathrooms.)

BEWILDERED
(Turning back to hand over tickets) This a side gig? Seems fun. You probably get free movies, too.

DISGRUNTLED
Sure.

(BEWILDERED has turned attention back to GIRL and doesn't hear.)

SARCASTIC
He's unaware of our circumstances.

DISGRUNTLED
Improbable.

BEWILDERED
(Returning focus to take tickets back) What is?

DISGRUNTLED
Cunning sacked me.

SARCASTIC
He fired us BOTH. And about three other clerks. Don't say you didn't know.

BEWILDERED
(Taken aback) I didn't! Yes, I give him a Layoff list. But neither of your names was on it.

DISGRUNTLED
Sure.

SARCASTIC
And our names are ...?

BEWILDERED
Listen. There's nothing to be done tonight. But I promise to straighten out this mess first thing Monday morning.

(BEWILDERED waves to YOUNG GIRL)

Come on, baby. (They exit UL.)

                    DISGRUNTLED
Can we trust him?

                    SARCASTIC
Friend, I can't even trust you.

        (YOUNG MAN and YOUNG LADY enter SR. YOUNG MAN crosses C. YOUNG
        LADY crosses to exit SL, bathrooms.)

                    YOUNG LADY
Go ahead in. Pick out seats.

                    YOUNG MAN
I'll wait here.

                    YOUNG LADY
Fine. I'll hurry. (She exits)

                    YOUNG MAN
        (To DISGRUNTLED and SARCASTIC as he hands tickets)

Has either of you seen *Evil Lurks Around the Corner*?

                    SARCASTIC
Not technically.

                    DISGRUNTLED
Though we have seen Evil enter that door.

        (YOUNG MAN pauses, confused.)

                    YOUNG MAN
I hope I chose the right movie, that's all. Scary enough to make her cuddle in, but not so
scary she gets tearful and wants to vanish.

                    DISGRUNTLED
The Forest Guardians is playing in Theater II. That sounds mildly scary to me.

                    YOUNG MAN
Isn't that animated? I'm hoping for romance not cuteness.

        (DISGRUNTLED shrugs)

YOUNG MAN, Cont.
Maybe I'll just reread the movie posters. (He exits SR.)

(WOMAN and ELDERLY MAN enter UL.)

ELDERLY MAN
I am going to the bathroom BY MYSELF. (She holds cane out.) And WITHOUT that
RIDICULOUS STICK!

WOMAN
Fine. But don't linger. If you're not back in your seat in 5 minutes, I'm coming after you.

(ELDERLY MAN crosses to exit SL. WOMAN exits UL.)

DISGRUNTLED
Speaking of lurking.

SARCASTIC
Please. If I get so old that people worry I can't go to the bathroom on my own … just end
it.

(EMT enters SR in time to hear her. Crosses C.)

EMT
(Handing SARCASTIC ticket and a pamphlet)

There's a Hot Line # on there to call if you ever want to talk with someone.

(YOUNG MAN reenters SR. Stops DR.)

DISGRUNTLED
(Amusedly pointing UR as SARCASTIC violently tears ticket)

Your movie is playing in Theater I.

(EMT exits UR. YOUNG LADY enters SL. Meets YOUNG MAN DC.)

YOUNG LADY
I hope this movie is not TOO scary. (They cross to exit UR.) Or sad. I hate sad movies.

(DISGRUNTLED and SARCASTIC each cross US to close curtains over doors.
They face US. Sounds/Music can be heard from theatres. ELDERLY MAN enters
SL. Sees Cat Flier. Takes it. Crosses to exit SR. DISGRUNTLED and SARCASTIC
return C.)

DISGRUNTLED
Finally. Peace and …

SARCASTIC
(As Sounds from movies increase)

... NOT Quiet.

(YOUNG MAN enters UR and crosses to exit SR.)

SARCASTIC
Don Juan on a Raisinets Quest.

(YOUNG GIRL enters UL and crosses to exit SL.)

DISGRUNTLED
Brutus's daughter. ... You never told me he had a daughter.

SARCASTIC
I just met the man! We aren't Instagram chums!

(WOMAN enters from UL and crosses C.)

WOMAN
(To them collectively.) Have you seen my father?

DISGRUNTLED and SARCASTIC
The old man?   Didn't he go to the bathroom?
I saw him go into the bathroom earlier.   I don't remember seeing him come out.

WOMAN
(Stopping them and pointing to DISGRUNTLED)

You. Please go into the Men's room and look for him.

(DISGRUNTLED exits SL. Awkward silence as WOMAN and SARCASTIC stare after. YOUNG MAN returns from SR with snacks. He crosses C to stand beside SARCASTIC and stare off, too.)

YOUNG MAN
What are you looking at?

SARCASTIC
(Jumping with a small shriek) The entrance to the bathrooms. This Woman's father may be lost.

YOUNG MAN
In the bathrooms? (Realizing, to WOMAN) The Woman from the Park! That old man is lost AGAIN?

WOMAN

Probably.

SARCASTIC

Maybe he's in Theater I. Why don't you two go look. I will wait here in case he's found in
the bathroom.

YOUNG MAN

(Hesitant to get involved) Okay.

> (YOUNG MAN exits UR. WOMAN follows him. YOUNG GIRL enters SL. Notices
> that flier is gone.)

YOUNG GIRL

(To SARCASTIC) I put a "Lost Cat" flier up here. Did you take it down?

SARCASTIC

No. But I should have. You can't just put fliers up anywhere you want to.

YOUNG GIRL

Did you see who did?

SARCASTIC

I don't spy…

> (YOUNG GIRL rushes C to grab SARCASTIC.)

YOUNG GIRL

Come on!

> YOUNG GIRL exits SR, pulling SARCASTIC with her. BEWILDERED enters UL
> and CUNNING enters UR. They cross C.

CUNNING

My Winner! That was some game this afternoon! Can't thank you enough. Buy you an
ICEE?

BEWILDERED

That's alright. I'm just looking for my daughter.

CUNNING

How old?

BEWILDERED

Almost nine.

CUNNING
And she's wandering around alone? What if she gets lost?

BEWILDERED
She just went to the bathroom. She's probably still in there.

(DISGRUNTLED returns SL.)

DISGRUNTLED
If you two are plotting a hostile takeover, you can have this place. I quit!

BEWILDERED
Did you see a young girl in there?

DISGRUNTLED
I was in the MEN's room, looking for a lost MAN. I was NOT in the WOMEN's room, looking for a lost CHILD. Child? Wow. It's as bad here as at Winkles. Maybe we should lock this place down, too.

(WOMAN and EMT enter UR.)

WOMAN
(To DISGRUNTLED) You're back! Did you find him?

DISGRUNTLED
No. I found a disaster in there, which I am NOT cleaning up! But no old man. (Softer) Sorry.

EMT
(To WOMAN) Check the Concessions stand, then the parking lot. Maybe he wandered off to your car. I'll check the Women's room, just in case he got mixed up.

(WOMAN exits SR. CUNNING follows. EMT starts to exit SL. BEWILDERED crosses to EMT.)

BEWILDERED
My daughter may be in there, too. Please look for me?

EMT
Of course. (Shaking head as exits SL) These people could lose their heads… .

(YOUNG MAN and YOUNG LADY enter UR. She waves at BEWILDERED.)

YOUNG LADY
Hi! Where's munchkin? (Overzealously) We had SO much fun stuffing bears last weekend!

BEWILDERED
(In a daze) Yes. Oh, hello. Yes, she's drags that purple stuffie everywhere. Thank you for
…. I'm not actually certain where she is right now. She said she was going to the
bathroom …

EMT
(Returning from SL) There's no one in either bathroom. I checked both.

YOUNG LADY
She's missing?!

YOUNG MAN
No way. That girl is street savvy.

BEWILDERED
(Crossing towards SR exit) Maybe she smelled popcorn.

  (He is stopped at the entrance. CUNNING and WOMAN return SR. SARCASTIC
  follows with a chair. WOMAN sits. EMT crosses to her.)

EMT
Ma'am, are you alright?

CUNNING
She's having a panic attack. I can empathize. It can be hard to hold so much
responsibility.

  (YOUNG GIRL and ELDERLY MAN return SR.)

BEWILDERED and WOMAN
YOU DISAPPEARED!

  (BEWILDERED rushes to GIRL and sweeps her up. WOMAN rushes to ELDERLY
  MAN and hugs him. She and EMT guide MAN carefully into chair. SARCASTIC
  exits SR.)

BEWILDERED
(Still tightly holding YOUNG GIRL) Do you realize how frightened I was?

ELDERLY MAN
(To BEWILDERED) Don't scold the child. It's my doing. She came looking for me.

  (SARCASTIC returns with Juice for ELDERLY MAN.)

WOMAN
(To Young Girl) Thank you, sweet girl. How did you know he was missing? Or where to
look?

YOUNG GIRL

Someone took the Cat Flier. It had to have been him. I knew he was out there looking for his Cat.

WOMAN

(Resigning to a decision) Then I will have to find her for him, won't I?

YOUNG MAN

But I thought the Cat was …

(YOUNG LADY puts finger on lips to shush him.)

SARCASTIC

I think *finding* his Cat is a wonderful idea.

ELDERLY MAN

(To WOMAN) It's alright, Natalie. My cat, Stormy, is dead.

WOMAN

You remember. …And you called me by *my* name, not *mom's*.

ELDERLY MAN

Sometimes I remember. Most times … I'm confused. … I'm sorry. … I miss those who have left. I sometimes feel … alone.

NATALIE

I think … all of us … at some time … feels alone. (Others nod in agreement) But, I'm right here by you, dad. … Charles.

CHARLES

Of course, you are.

NATALIE

I'm sorry I get impatient. … I love you … Maybe you'd like to find a *new* cat?

CHARLES

With you, daughter, yes. Very much.

BEWILDERED

(After a tearful pause, to CUNNING)

Perhaps two new *executive* positions at Winkles (nodding his attention to Disgruntled and Sarcastic) could also be *'found'* today?

(DISGRUNTLED and SARCASTIC look at CUNNING. Others look at him, too. Moment of silence.)

CUNNING

(Caving) Fine. (Happy reactions) I'll just need their names.

SARCASTIC and DISGRUNTLED
Teri   Terry

(They look at each other in delighted surprise.)

BEWILDERED

(To CUNNING) Thank you, (Mr./Ms.) Winkle. (He hugs his daughter.) I'm proud of you, too, dear.

CUNNING

Call me Peyton. …And you *should* be proud of…

YOUNG GIRL

…Emily. I'm Emily. And this is my dad. Ben.

PEYTON

You should be proud of Emily, …Ben. And of yourself. I see that I haven't give you enough credit.

(PEYTON, BEN, EMILY cross to exits for respective movies.)

YOUNG MAN

(To YOUNG LADY) I'm Sam.

YOUNG LADY

I know, silly.

SAM

Well, everyone was introducing themselves, so I thought … (YOUNG LADY kisses him.)

YOUNG LADY

Colby.

(She wraps her arm around his and pulls him into movie.)

CHARLES

(To WOMAN as he stands) On that note … we, too, have a movie to finish.

NATALIE

(Kindly) Unless you'd prefer to visit the Humane Society.

CHARLES

Oh! I would like that very much. (To EMT, who has begun to leave.) THANK YOU …

EMT
...Jordan. My pleasure. Take care of each other.

(EMT exits to movie. CHARLES and NATALIE exit SR. TERRY and TERI are
now the only people left in the lobby. Pause. Realization.)

TERRY and TERI
What are we wearing these for?   What are we standing here for?

(They rip off movie complex vests & run off SR.)

(Lights down.)

What My Mom Doesn't Say
Finalist in the Derick Burleson Poetry Contest

Elly Katz

She wears paragraphs on her face,
streams of soundless sentences steady there in
reeds of muscles at cheek bones,
hiking the capsized hill of a chin,
skewing the balance of lenses across
the bridge of the nose.

It's all there— screwed tight in
measured
buckets of loss.

Menisci rupture,
surface-tension crying
with overflow.

Prayers go unaddressed,
marked with missing postage or
accidentally mailed to the wrong God.

Her face is sentinel to my face,
to what I cannot face,
what I must efface, if only for a
heartbeat.

Here, wear this for me—
a trillion tons of grief sinking me,
I didn't have to beg
across the silence.

Yes, that's how I will breathe,
even if I seethe.

I will carry that too,
she didn't have to say, because her
speechlessness said it
before the longing crossed
grooves inside me.

Buckeye in the Prairie Patch
Finalist in the Mary Cassatt Art Contest

Karen Colstrom

All Under One Sky
3rd Place in the Susan Hansell Drama Contest

One-Act Play
Sherrie Pesta

CHARACTERS
>   Hannah (F, mid 20's – mid 30's) … mom
>   Alex (M, mid 20's – mid 30's) … dad #1
>   Julian (M, late 30's – early 40's) … dad #2
>   Bonnie (F, 10-12) … daughter
>   Alan (M, 8-10) … son

SETTING
>   Four Lawn Chairs. Two sit CR, facing DSL; two sit CL, facing DSR. A cooler is
>   placed C, serving as a sort of table. There are bags on either end of the line to hold
>   props.

Scene One

(It's July, 1969, near Cape Canaveral, Florida. HANNA sits in the far SR chair,
beside BONNIE, SRC. ALEX sits in the far SL chair, beside ALAN, SLC. The
children are dressed in jean shorts with off white t-shirts and tennis shoes or flip
flops. The parents reflect late 1960's fashion. Snacks, cameras, perhaps a small
radio, may be seen. It's early morning. As lights rise, music might provide context
of time.)

ALAN

How long do we have to sit here?

ALEX

Until the rocket launches. It shouldn't be much longer.

BONNIE

You should have brought something to do. *(She draws on a pad or Etch-a-sketch)* Like I
did.

HANNAH

(To Alan) You don't want to miss this, sweetie. America is making history today.

ALAN

(Brief pause) But I'm hungry.

                                BONNIE
You're always hungry.

                                HANNAH
        (Passing him a pop tart)

Try not to eat too fast.

                                ALEX
Is that the last pop tart?

                                HANNAH
Yes. Let him have it. He's growing tall. You're only growing wide.

                                ALEX

Cheerios?

        (HANNAH shakes 'no').

Bugles?

                                HANNAH
Gone. I promise to make you a hearty lunch.

                                ALEX

A bologna sandwich. With mayo.

                                HANNAH
If that's what you want.

                                ALEX
Hand me the coffee thermos, at least.

        (HANNAH does.)

Maybe we should have gotten a sitter.

                                HANNAH
I want to see their faces when the rocket lifts. A mother wants to see their children explore
the world.

                                ALEX
They could have watched it on television. (Pause) Did you bring the camera?

        (She pulls it out and hands it to him.)

Is there film in it?

                                HANNAH
Brand new cannister.

          (She turns to BONNIE)

What are you drawing?

                                BONNIE
(Beaming) The rocket. Isn't it amazing?

                                HANNAH
          (Throwing an "I told you so" look at ALEX)

Your drawing is amazing, too, Bonnie. Maybe you'll go to Art School one day.

                                ALAN
I'm HOT.

                                BONNIE
It's Florida. In July. (To Mom) I want to go to the moon one day.

                                ALAN
Girls can't go to the moon.

                                HANNAH
Times are changing. A woman today can do and be anything she wishes.

                                ALEX
Realistically…

                                HANNAH
Anything!

                                ALAN
Dad went to college! Didn't you, Dad.

                                ALEX
(Proudly) I certainly did! Two years at Rollins College studying Business. That's why I'm
a successful shop manager today.

                                BONNIE
Did you go to college, mom?

                                HANNAH
I wanted to. I wanted to study education, be a teacher.

BONNIE

Why didn't you?

HANNAH

My father didn't see the point in a woman going to college.

ALEX

(To Bonnie) Your mom didn't need a degree. We became engaged in high school. Her father knew I would take care of her.

    (Silence.)

BONNIE

Well, I'm going to college.

HANNAH

Of course, you are.

ALEX

We'll see when the time comes.

ALAN
    (Conveniently interrupting the awkward silence.)

Dad, do you think the astronauts will meet someone on the moon?

BONNIE

(Laughing) Who? A little green man? I suppose you also think the moon is made of cheese.

ALAN

Ooh! Cheese!

ALEX

I doubt there are people...or little green men...on the moon, Alan. But, even if there are, *our MEN* will plant the American flag on the moon's surface and claim it for our beautiful country, home of the free.

    (HANNAH is trying to get reception on radio.)

HANNAH

Alex, SHUSH! The countdown!

    (ALEX does not like being shushed. They stare at sky in silence. HANNAH may hand binoculars to kids.)

                                    ALEX
Blast off!

                                    BONNIE
It's going SO HIGH!

                                    ALAN
            (Eyes still looking upwards)

I need to go to the bathroom.

                                    BONNIE
I wonder if any of the astronauts are afraid of heights.

                                    ALAN
Men are not afraid of anything.

                                    BONNIE
(To Mom) Will they be gone long? I feel bad for the moms and children left behind.

                                    ALAN
I want to take a picture.

                                    BONNIE
You'd break the camera.

            (A few more moments of silence before they look down.)

                                    HANNAH
I'm breathless.

                                    ALEX
That was a fine, patriotic sight.

                                    ALAN
Can we go now?

                                    ALEX
            (Standing, to Alan)

Come on, son. Let's find you a bathroom while the girls pack up.

            (Lights down.)

Scene Two

(It's March, 1997, near Phoenix, Arizona. HANNAH has made a slight costume change to reflect time and has moved into SRC chair. BONNIE has moved out to SR. She wears a sweater, cap, tennis shoes. ALAN has moved to SL chair, wearing a sweatshirt, cap, tennis shoes. JULIAN, in attire reflecting the late 1990s, has replaced ALEX, in SLC chair. He has an expensive camera with tripod, etc. It's evening, between 9 and 10 PM. Several pairs of binoculars may still be out. Remains of a picnic are on cooler. As lights gradually rise, music might help set mood / time.)

ALAN

Why do we have to sit here? The campground has a pool.

HANNAH

It's too cold to swim at night, Alan. Maybe if it warms up tomorrow… .

BONNIE

You should have brought something to do.

(She has a portable cassette player and headphones)

I did.

JULIAN

We've been hiking all day, little man. Aren't you exhausted? And don't forget why we came to Arizona.

ALAN

To see little *green* men.

JULIAN

UFO's. Unidentified Flying Objects. This is supposed to be the place to see them. Aren't you curious?

ALAN

I'm hungry.

BONNIE

You're always hungry.

(HANNAH offers string cheese.)

ALAN

And thirsty! It's so dry out here.

(JULIAN gives him a juice box.)

                                  BONNIE
It's Arizona.

                                  HANNAH
Do you have the fliers, Julian? I'm not sure what I'm looking for.

                                  JULIAN
                (Handing her a colorful brochure)

Could be anything out of the ordinary. A saucer-like shape. Flashing lights. The Park
Ranger said he has seen countless unexplained occurrences.

                                  BONNIE
I want to be a Park Ranger one day. It's so peaceful and quiet out here.

                (She bobs to her music.)

                                  HANNAH
How can you tell, dear? Cut that music down before you harm your ears.

                                  ALAN
Girls can't be Park Rangers. Only MEN are strong enough to fight off a bear or coyote.

                                  JULIAN
                (Pointing up the trail)

Actually, there are two female Park Rangers just ahead. Women can do and be anything
they wish to.

                                  ALAN
I suppose.

                                  BONNIE
Look at Mom! She's a successful Engineer.

                                  JULIAN
                (With a tad of jealousy?)

That's right. An MIT graduate, surpassing most men in the field.

                                  HANNAH
(Overcompensating) No more successful than my award-winning, photojournalist,
husband!

                                  JULIAN
I have just been lucky. Been at the right places at the right time. I could not afford
university tuition.

HANNAH

Yet look what you have done with natural talent and determination! Your photos are nationally syndicated!

JULIAN

Maybc I'll be in the right place at the right time today, too.

(Switching conversation to son)

What do you think an alien looks like, Alan? I bet they have six arms and four eyes. What a photo shoot that could be!

BONNIE

They probably look a lot like us. ... Though maybe less fashionable.

ALAN

Maybe we should save some of the string cheese. So, they can eat IT. Instead of US.

(Pause. Laughter)

I need to go to the bathroom.

HANNAH

If you leave the safety of our circle, aren't you afraid an alien might abduct you?

ALAN

I'm not afraid of anything. I'd *like* to ride in a spaceship. See an alien planet.

BONNIE

Mom, do scientists believe in aliens?

HANNAH

Well.... Belief is a personal...

BONNIE

... I don't want to be abducted. I don't want to leave you behind, Mom! Dad, wouldn't you feel sad?

ALAN

They'd still have me.

BONNIE

Sad.

(Lights suddenly flash across the stage, and they all look towards the sky. Gasps. Long Pause. Then they begin to whisper to one another.

                                    HANNAH
I didn't *believe*… we would really see….

                                    JULIAN
                (Shooting pictures wildly with a professional camera)

… I don't know what that is …

                                    HANNAH
Does that look like a 'v'?

                                    ALAN
IT'S A SHIP!

                                    BONNIE
With flashing lights!

                                    ALAN
Take a picture of me with it!

                                    BONNIE
You'd break the camera.

                (They stare. Pause. They look down.)

                                    JULIAN
Wow. I was not expecting that.

                                    HANNAH
                (Standing. To ALAN)

Come on, sweetheart.

                (She snatches camera from JULIAN)

I'll take a picture of you on the edge of that field while your sister and dad start to pack
up.

                                    ALAN
Can I take a picture myself?

                                    HANNAH
                (Looking at JULIAN, she hands expensive camera to son)

Sure.

ALAN

(Holding camera recklessly, Alan runs off)

Yea!

(HANNAH follows as Lights go down.)

Scene Three

(It's January, 2023, on the deck of an Alaskan Cruise Ship. BONNIE and ALAN return to C chairs. They are now covered in blankets. They wear coats, hats, gloves. JULIAN has moved to SL chair and is similarly covered for the cold weather. ALEX has replaced HANNAH in SR chair, also dressed warmly, and covered with a blanket. All have cameras and mugs of hot chocolate. It's around midnight. For a moment, they all stare silently into the sky. ALEX and JULIAN are obviously delighted. BONNIE and ALAN have begun to get bored and tired. As lights rise, music might indicate time and place.)

BONNIE

How long do we have to sit quietly. It's been hours.

JULIAN

It's been twenty minutes. Twenty glorious minutes!

ALAN

You should have brought something to do.

(Pulls out a Gameboy)

Like I did.

(Begins to play.)

ALEX

Put that away! We are here to experience the Northern Lights, together! Not play a video game.

ALAN

(Alan grumpily puts it away. Pause.)

I'm hungry.

BONNIE

You're always hungry. The buffet is closed. They need time to restock because of you.

ALAN

And I'm FREEZING.

                              BONNIE
It's Alaska. In January.

        (Starting to agree with ALAN.)

And we're sitting on a boat deck, surrounded by ICE. At MIDNIGHT!

                              JULIAN
(To ALEX) Perhaps it is time for the kids to retire.

                              ALEX
And miss this once-in-a-lifetime opportunity?

                              ALAN
I'm not a kid.

                              ALEX
SEE! They can handle a little cold for just a bit longer.

        (To BONNIE and ALAN)

Where are the polaroids I bought you? Maybe you'll catch a whale in your photo. Or a
polar bear.

                              JULIAN
In the dark?

        (ALEX shushes him)

                              BONNIE
I want to *save* the Polar Bears one day.

                              JULIAN
Admirable!

                              ALAN
One 'girl' can't save an entire species.

                              JULIAN
One 'GIRL' can change the world!

        (Silent pause as they continue to watch. BONNIE and ALAN take pictures with
        their polaroids.)

                              ALAN
What are the lights? They look like fire.

ALEX

Ask your father. He's the one with the Doctorate in Mythology.

BONNIE

They look like they are dancing. Maybe the stars are dancing!

JULIAN

According to myth, the Aurora Borealis is a visualization of ancestral *spirits* dancing near earth.

BONNIE

I don't like spirits. ...Are they evil? ... They look so pretty.

JULIAN

Ask your father. He has the Doctorate in Religion.

ALEX

They are said to be the spirits of family members. I don't *believe* they are evil.

BONNIE

Spirits who don't want to leave? That is sad.

ALEX

Or spirits watching over us. Which can be comforting.

JULIAN

(About ALEX as well as the stars)

Beautiful.

BONNIE

When Alan and I are older, do we have to get Doctorates, too?

JULIAN

Only if you wish to.

ALAN

Do we HAVE to go to college at all?

ALEX and JULIAN

YES!

ALEX

At least get a Bachelor's. The world has become a competitive place.

JULIAN

A Master's wouldn't hurt.

ALAN

(After a groan) I need to go to the bathroom.

JULIAN

(Ignoring him) There is another story, a Finnish tale about the lights. They call them 'fox fires', and claim they are started by a Firefox whose tail flings sparks when he runs.

ALAN

I like that story! I told you they look like a fire.

(ALAN cuddles deep into his blanket to fall asleep.)

BONNIE

I like the fox better than dead people, too. Maybe he dances while he runs.

(She cuddles in to sleep, too.)

ALEX

Shouldn't we tell them the truth, the scientific causes of the lights?

JULIAN

They have plenty of time for truths. Let them enjoy fantasy for a while longer.

ALEX

Marrying you remains the best decision I have ever made.

JULIAN

You mean besides adopting those two?

ALEX

Naturally.

JULIAN

Ours is a stars-in-the-sky, kind of story.

(JULIAN and ALEX stare at the sky.)

(Lights go down.)

Snow Home
Finalist in the Derick Burleson Poetry Contest

Dave Malone

Red-tailed hawk puffs up
on the utility pole
in the January freeze.

We lock eyes, turn beaks,
then I tromp
through snowdrifts

en route to the far end
of the yard to build a home.
I fashion heavy bricks

from Mother's baking pans
I've stolen though she'll not notice.
I pluck out perfect blocks

with Father's slide rule
he'll never use again.
When I've got the dome completed,

it's time to bring in the sleeping bag
and the neighbor's shell of a dog.
Here we sleep through the afternoon

while the wind hugs our snow home,
and the raptor takes a field mouse
against a gentle whooshing of sleet.

Autumn Enchantment
Finalist in the Mary Cassatt Art Contest

Karen Colstrom

Reconsider
Finalist in the Derick Burleson Poetry Contest

Megan Munger

As the sun sets at 9:33 PM on June 26th, I ask it
to reconsider. I glance into black bushes
and remain silent, a predator, as the sky turns

Cabernet. Reconsider because I'm not yet done
with today. I've spend it here on this patio
reading, writing in baby blue pen, trying
to enjoy being broke down a dirt road,

unprepared for everything. I need more time
on one of the longest days of the year,
how outrageous am I, but darkness isn't
the same out here without streetlights.

The only sound is the cows as they move
into their barn for the night. Darkness isn't
a shroud to clothe my flaws like it used to be.

When we met at the college park, my high school
boyfriend asked me, *have you ever reconsidered?*
All he wanted was for me to come back, to be his girl.

Unlike when we were sixteen, he had money,
time, a better understanding, more
maturity. He made it sound easy—why
can't I just leave, go be with him in the city?
With our new cars, graduations soon,

it would be perfect timing, accomplished
like we always promised. When I got up
to leave, it felt like it does out here tonight. Wrong

and why did I come here? I want
to go home. I need to go apologize
for the pain I've caused, reconsider
my safety in the arms of a man I met
ten days after we broke up. I've loved him

and stayed here ever since. Reconsider how
the night sky makes me feel like Macbeth's wife.
Reconsider how I turn the key to lock us in.

Swedish Country Charm
Finalist in the Mary Cassatt Art Contest

Karen Colstrom

Territorial
Finalist in the Derick Burleson Poetry Contest

Franziska Roesner

It rains so much this spring that
even the houses start growing,
sprouting windows where there had
been siding, bulbs bursting
into new rooms, carpeted as though with
pollen, spiral staircases wrapping
like vines and breaking
through attics, shingles hurrying,
fern-like, to fill in the gaps.
Monstrous and beautiful like
a strangely bulbed strawberry, like
a blackberry branch reaching, rooting
overnight in the next yard over.
When the rains pass, do we weed it?
Do we leave? Or can we stay?

Monarch in Flora
Finalist in the Mary Cassatt Art Contest

Karen Colstrom

Unmoored
Finalist in the Derick Burleson Poetry Contest

Franziska Roesner

I don't believe in prayer but
I wish I did. I wish I had

understood that my parents, too,
would get older, that my father's

limbs would stop responding
well, a kink in the neural hose

slowing water to a dribble,
that my mother's face would slowly

fold in upon itself like a
wet newspaper, that they

would watch for signs of their own
unmooring, that they

wouldn't mention any of this
to me.

Reflections of Fall
Finalist in the Mary Cassatt Art Contest

Karen Colstrom

Trumpeter Swan
Finalist in the Mary Cassatt Art Contest

Karen Colstrom

Asemic Text w285
Finalist in the Mary Cassatt Art Contest

Gregory Stump

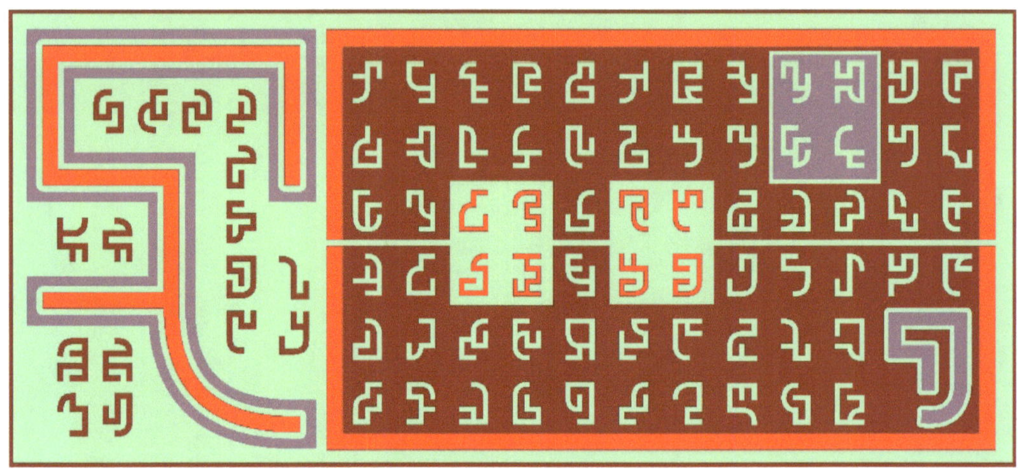

Asemic Text w338
Finalist in the Mary Cassatt Art Contest

Gregory Stump

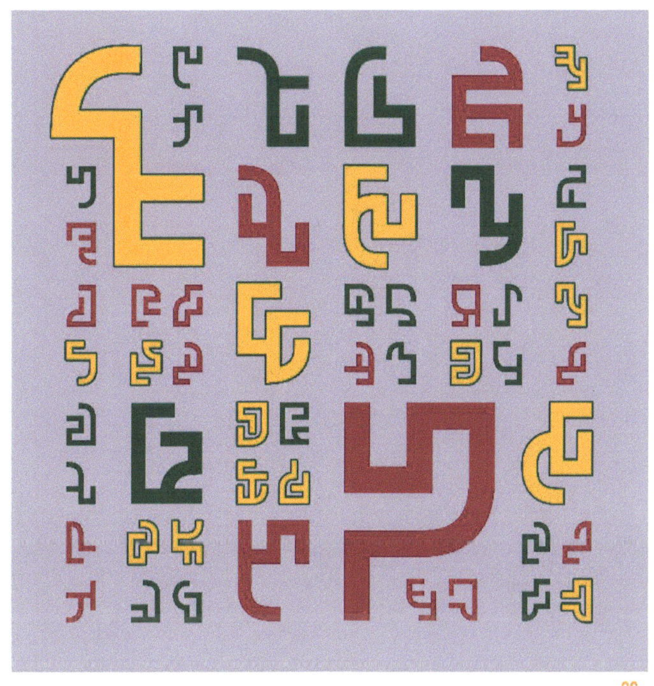

Asemic Text w347
Finalist in the Mary Cassatt Art Contest

Gregory Stump

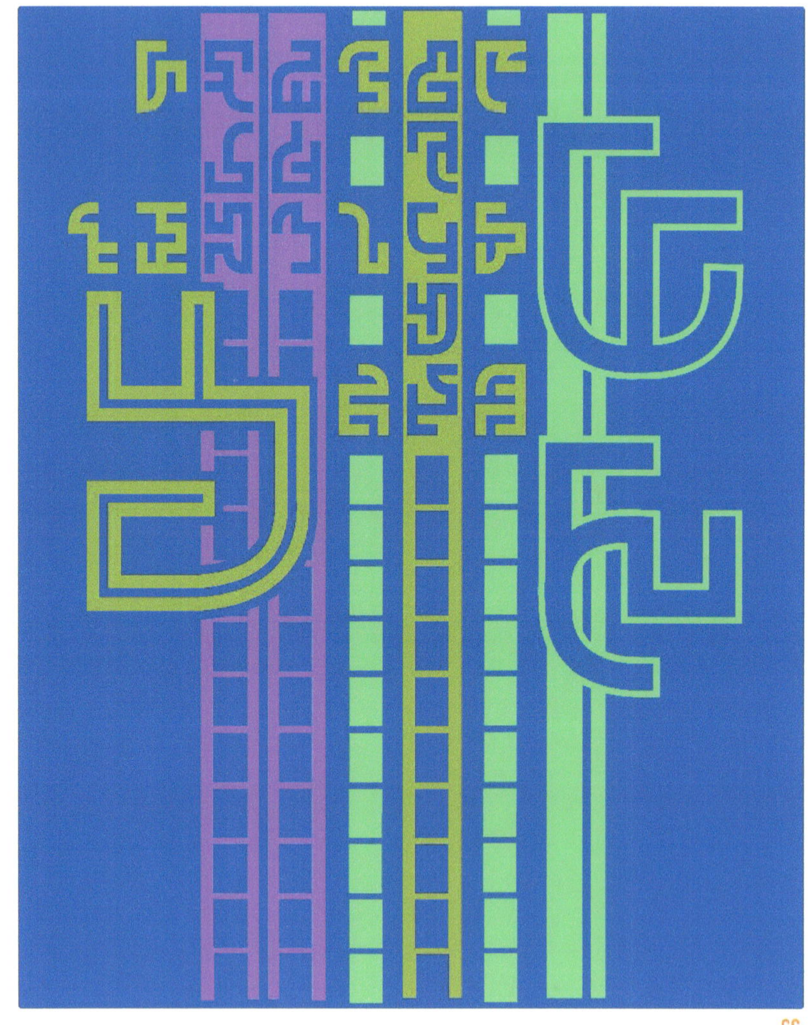

Central Europe #3f
Finalist in the Mary Cassatt Art Contest

Kenneth Kesner

Eastern Europe #12g
Finalist in the Mary Cassatt Art Contest

Kenneth Kesner

Christine Andersen is a retired dyslexia specialist who hikes daily in the Connecticut woods, pen and pad in pocket, hounds at her heels. Many of her poems are inspired by the outdoors. Publications include *The Comstock Review, The Octillo Review, Awakenings Review, Gyroscope Review, Evening Street Review, SLAB, The Dewdrop, Glimpse, DASH, Rushing through the Dark,* and *Glassworks*, among others. She won the 2023 *American Writers Review* Poetry Contest.

Brian C. Billings is a professor of drama and English at Texas A&M University-Texarkana and the editor-in-chief for *Aquila Review*, the university's literary journal. In addition to managing TAMU-T's drama program, he teaches courses in drama, creative writing, and children's literature. His work has appeared in such journals as *Antietam Review, Ancient Paths, Argestes, Backstreet Quarterly, Confrontation, Evening Street Review, Poems and Plays,* and *Rushing Thru the Dark.* Publishers for his scripts include Eldridge Publishing and Heuer Publishing. For more information about his work, please contact him at brianbillings625@gmail.com.

Karen Colstrom is a native-born Kansan who grew up on the farm. She has a background in art, graduating from Emporia State University. Karen taught a children's program for 20 years, sharing her love of art. Her current passion is photography on the family farm. Karen's photography is inspired by the beauty of nature. She has a website: prairiedesignphotography.com.

Jenn Dean holds an MFA from the Bennington Writing Seminars. She's been published in *Salamander, Hawaii Pacific Review,* and *The Writer's Chronicle,* among others. Her long-form essay, *The Keepers of the Ghost Bird*, published through *Massachusetts Review's* Working Titles series as an e-book, won the 2018 John Burroughs Nature Essay Award. The essay is anthologized in *When Birds Are Near* (Cornell U. Press). A former member of BirdNote.org's production team, she hosted their tour of the Galapagos. She's working on a nonfiction essay collection called *Letters from the Valley of the Moon*, chronicling aspects of the Snoqualmie Valley.

Frank William Finney is a poet from Massachusetts. A Joint winner of The Letter Review Prize for Poetry, his poems have been published by *Blue Unicorn, Drawn to the Light Press, Glacial Hills Review, Persephone Literary Magazine,* and elsewhere. His chapbook *The Folding of the Wings* was published in 2022 (FLP Books).

Susan Harrison is a retired attorney. In 2016, she published a historical novel set in Pakistan, *Beneath a Shooting Star,* under the pseudonym Susan Harrison Rashid. The novel was a 2017 finalist for four awards, including the Connecticut Book Award. She currently lives in Connecticut with her husband.

Greta Holt is the recipient of two Ohio Arts Council Individual Artist Fellowships in fiction. She has published stories in literary magazines and anthologies, including the *Southern Indiana Review, Tulip Tree Review, A Plate of Pandemic,* and *What Mennonites Are Thinking.* Her website is: https://gretaholtwriter.com. She is working on a collection about Botswana, where her parents worked as educators in the early 1980s.

Victoria James is a high school English and Creative Writing teacher. She was awarded a Masters of Science in Secondary Education and a Masters of the Arts in Literature from Pitt State University. Victoria is currently a reader for *Emerald City Literary Magazine* and *Cow Creek Review* while working on her Creative Writing emphasis at Pittsburg State University. Her fiction appears in *Coneflower Café*, Spring 2023 and *Cow Creek Review 2024*. Her poetry appears in *Cow Creek Review's 2023 and 2024 volume, Empyrean Literary Magazine's Volume 6 and Volume 8, Mindful Phoenix's Volume I: The Coping Day to Day*, and *1134's The Archivist*.

Elly Katz, at 27, verging towards a doctorate at Harvard went to a doctor for mundane procedure to stabilize her neck. Upon waking from anesthesia, she searched in vain for the right half of her body. Somehow, she survived what doctors surmised was unsurvivable: a brainstem stroke secondary to a physician's needle misplacement. Her path towards science, amongst other ambitions, came to a halt. As a devout writer, she feared that poetry, too, fell outside what was possible given her inert right fingers. However, in the wake of tragedy, she discovered the power of dictation and the bounty of metaphor.

Kenneth Kesner (肯内思) splits his time between the Caucasus and South East Asia. Some recent works are featured in: *Levitate Magazine, New Note Poetry, Poetry Pacific, October Hill Magazine* and *Wayne Literary Review*.

Dave Malone is a poet and playwright who lives in the Missouri Ozarks. He spent his early childhood in Riley, Kansas, and later graduated from Olathe North High School. He holds degrees from Ottawa University and Indiana State University. A three-time Pushcart nominee, he is the author of eight collections of poetry, most recently *Bypass* (Kelsay Books, 2023). His work has been featured on NPR and appeared in *Midwest Review, San Pedro River Review,* and *Red Rock Review*. He offers a free monthly e-newsletter. More at *davemalone.net*.

Patrick Manning teaches composition in the Department of English at the University of Pittsburgh. He also serves as the Outreach Director in the university's Writing Center. Patrick's critical writing has appeared in *Community Literacy Journal, The Canadian Journal of American Studies, Journal of the Midwest MLA* and elsewhere, and his creative writing has appeared in various places, including the edited collection *Western Pennsylvania Reflections: Stories from the Alleghenies to Lake Erie.* Patrick lives in Pittsburgh with his spouse and two children.

Glenn Moss is a media lawyer and has been writing poetry and stories since high school. At Binghamton University, he wrote a play for a course in Jacobean Literature, and at Case Western Reserve Law School, he wrote a play for a course in Jurisprudence. Returning to NYC, Glenn writes poetry and stories amidst contracts. Each enriches the other, with contracts benefiting from a bit of poetic dance. Glenn has had poems and stories published in *Ithaca Lit, West Trade Review,* Oddville Press, *Oberon, Foliate Oak Magazine, Illuminations, Qu, 34th Parallel, Harbinger's Asylum, Trolley Magazine, October Hill Magazine,* and *Narrative Northeast*.

Megan Munger is a Kansas poet and Pacific University MFA Candidate. She received her M.A. and B.S.Ed. in English from Pittsburg State University, where she received the James B.M. Schick *Midwest Quarterly* Graduate Studies Best Essay Award in 2021 and 2022. She currently resides in Junction City, KS, where she teaches English at Junction City High School. Her poetry has previously appeared in the *Of Our Own Accord* anthology by Flying Ketchup Press and online at *Kitchen Table Quarterly* and *The Coop: A Poetry Cooperative*.

Sherrie Pesta, PhD is a theatre educator and practitioner. Her previously published plays include: *Pencils, Paper, and Poison* with Heartland Plays (2019); *The Beach Umbrella* with Choeofpleirn Press (2021), a Susan Hansell Drama Prize winner; *Find a Penny with* Choeofpleirn Press (2022); and *The Hot House* with Nervous Ghost Press (2023). She recently enjoyed having a theatre-for-youth script, *The Mystery of the Missing Clauses*, produced by The Quannapowitt Players (2023).

Jordyn-Elizabeth Pimental is an honors college student studying Environmental Science in coastal Massachusetts. When she is not listening to the nearby Atlantic while paddleboarding or crafting stories while writing it is almost a guarantee she is taking pictures of birds. Having an obsession with the natural world, Jordyn is happy to express her love for the planet by taking pictures of it.

Andrea Reynolds is a high school English teacher from St. Louis who finished her MFA in 2021. She grew up roaming the neighborhoods of St. Louis city, but she enjoys spending her free time visiting family in Linn, Missouri. Her newest joy is a dog named Rigby.

Jane Richards' poetry has appeared in numerous journals, including *Glacial Hills Review, After Hours, Gyroscope Review,* and *Willow Review*. Her work has been included in *The Best of Choeofpleirn Press,* and she has been nominated for a Pushcart prize. Her chapbook, *The Feather Variations*, was published in spring, 2024. A retired piano teacher, she now pursues her life-long passions for writing, nature and travel. She holds masters degrees in social work and creative writing.

Franziska (Franzi) Roesner holds a PhD in computer science and is a professor at the University of Washington in Seattle, teaching and researching computer security and privacy. She was a poet before she was a computer scientist, though, and she has returned to poetry in the last few years. She lives in Seattle with her husband, two daughters, and one remaining cat. You can find her website at https://www.franziroesner.com/poetry.

Sara R. Sands, PhD, is an Instructional Associate Professor in Public Administration at the University of Houston. She earned a PhD in Politics & Education at Teachers College, Columbia University and a Master of Philosophy in Education at the University of Cambridge. She studied creative writing at Tulane University, where she completed a B.A. in English and Political Economy, and the New Orleans Center for Creative Arts. Her work has appeared in *American Chordata,* the *Arkansas Review: A Journal of Delta Studies,* and *The Merrimack Review*. She lives in Houston with her husband and a growing collection of houseplants.

Gregory Stump, an emeritus professor of linguistics, is a visual artist who currently works in digital media. His series of asemic artworks draws upon his long-standing interest in the graphic representation of language. He has provided cover art for books issued by Cambridge University Press, State Street Press, and Finishing Line Press. He resides in the Kansas City area. About the art: People often encounter text that they recognize as writing but whose words or symbols they cannot read. This is true of preliterate children, second-language learners, archaeologists examining undeciphered inscriptions, travelers to other countries, visitors to a museum's international collection, customers in Asian groceries or restaurants, and so on. One of the inspirations for the asemic artwork in Stump's portfolio is the unique state of mind shared by all of these people: an awareness that something is a text without any ability to read that text—a text whose immediate significance must be a matter of creative conjecture.

Annual Kenneth Johnston Nonfiction Book Contest
Submit your book length manuscript to
choeofpleirnpress@gmail.com.
Winner receives $300, free publication, 5 free copies of the print paperback,
and free advertising for a year.
Contest fee: $30
Follow submission details at
www.choeofpleirnpress.com/nonfiction-book-contest
See past winners and finalists a
www.choeofpleirnpress.com/bookstore

Jonathan Holden Poetry
Chapbook Contest
First Time Poets
Submit your poetry chapbooks of 25-40 pages
Between January 1 and April 30, 2025
$20 entry fee
Winning poet receives $200, 10 copies of the print
book, and free social media advertising
Follow our Submission Guidelines:
https://www.choeofpleirnpress.com/poetry-
chapbook-contest

Listening for Low Tide

Too much happens at ground level:
the kids selling candy or delivering
newspapers shortcut through the yard,
the neighbors' dogs blare their alarms
in unison, and teens, shielded by the heartbeat
of their music, speed down the street.

Two stories above the ground.
I welcome the afternoon sunlight
as it stretches across the rug,
my cat moving with it. From the opposite
window, the shadows cast by trees
overspread the ground, the sunlight only
hitting the treetops. Sound waves lap
against the building, the tide at its lowest
each night when the owl in the park
starts to hoot its presence.

Available at Amazon and
Choeofpleirn Press

Honorable Mention in the
Eric Hoffer Book Awards, 2024

Using the scientific process, Heflin re-examines ancient artifacts and myths from the ancient world to demonstrate how women's ties to the cosmos were honored and revered. From being able to bleed, but not die, for 3-5 days, to having menstrual cycles in sync with the moon--ancient women exercised Feminine Power, a power so fierce that modern patriarchists denigrate trans women and drag queens who have embraced it.

Learn why patriarchists want us to believe that patriarchies have always existed, when, in fact, they only arose after 2400 BCE, when Egyptians determined that males actually play a role in procreation.

The evidence is written for both lay and scholarly readers, so that everyone can learn the real truth.

Print copies are available wherever you buy books. The digital copy can be purchased through Choeofpleirn Press.

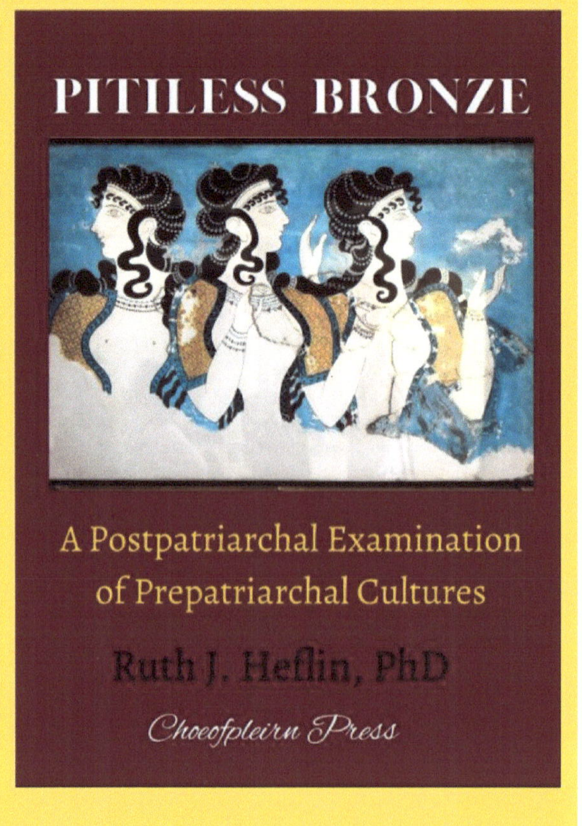

Inspired
by Kansas Poet Laureate

Traci Brimhall

Check out Choeofpleirn Press'
new zine, Harvest Harmonies,
where you can copy and share poetry-memes
from our 2024 contest winners.

Give the gift of poetry to the world.
https://www.choeofpleirnpress.com/harvest-
harmony-2024
The poem-memes are also available on our Facebook page.

FUN FACT

Choeofpleirn is a word James P. Cooper invented
by combining the letters of
our surnames alternately.
It's pronounced, "chuf-plern"
and loosely means
"the chief place of rest."

We hope you found the literature herein
restful and rejuvenating.

Choeofpleirn Press
A 501(c)3 nonprofit

THE BEST OF CHOEOFPLEIRN PRESS
Winter 2024
Copyright 2024

Produced in Kansas